nicROCKE

MARC SHERROD

Grey Wolfe Publishing, LLC
PO Box 1088
Birmingham, Michigan 48009
www.GreyWolfePublishing.com

© 2014 Marc Sherrod
Published by Grey Wolfe Publishing, LLC
www.GreyWolfePublishing.com
All Rights Reserved

ISBN: 978-1-628280593
Library of Congress Control Number: 2014957463

Nic Rocke

Marc Sherrod

Dedication

For all the Nic Rockes. You know who you are.

Prologue

Derek turned the knob, hoping the directions were correct. On the other side he expected to find a small chamber, the first of several, eventually leading to the main control room. He was not disappointed. Through the dim lighting he could make out the identification number on the far side of the room, which he quickly compared to the one listed on his map. "51B, medical facility, that's what I need," he muttered to no one. Immediately he felt the weight leave his shoulders as he leaned against the doorframe in relief. He glanced at the rip in his left side where the blade had raked him hardly an hour earlier. Coagulated blood caked his shirt, though the wound itself still oozed. He knew it was bad.

Pulling a dirty bottle from his sack, he drank the last few drops. Lack of water was a concern, but the problem with the gash in his body had to be addressed first. Hours with the med techs back home as part of his training, which he originally thought a waste of time, was actually proving to be useful. John, if he were still alive, would be wagging a finger at him with that "I told you so" look in his eyes. The fire, back before the maze, had taken care of John.

"Derek, its Anne. Are you still there?"

The voice over his com link was startling. He thought the girl had perished shortly after John in the lower catacombs. He had heard Anne scream. The Guardians down here were known to be merciless, and he had assumed she had been finished.

"Anne? Really, is that you?" he responded with a wearied voice. Doubt swiftly crossed his mind, along with a panicky flutter as he realized this could be one of the traps. Giving a response to a bugged com link was a death sentence, either by the fatal sound wave the Guardians would send back through his receiver or through the team they would dispatch to wander the halls; they would hunt him down and kill him. His reaction was one of instinct, and he cursed himself for having no control.

There were a few moments of silence, leaving Derek in dread. The sweat on his upper lip dropped down into his mouth, leaving a salty, oily taste. He could only imagine what he looked like now, a beaten, muddied shadow of the once proud fighter who was selected directly for training, and subsequently handpicked for this opportunity.

"Yes, Derek, it's me." The girl's response was enough to convince him. He didn't care how much human appearances could be mimicked, the central computer, for now, still couldn't emulate the human voice properly; something innate was always missing. Derek had decided it was because the central computer lacked a human soul.

"I barely escaped the Guardians," Anne continued. "One seared me with a fire stick and I fell. Maybe two floors, I don't know. My head struck something, I lost consciousness." Anne began to weep; the soft sobbing was clear through his receiver. "I'm scared Derek, they are all around here."

Derek slammed the wall in frustration. Worse than having to endure his own fears were listening to those of Anne, whom he was unable to help. Pain wrapped around his abdomen as he righted himself and began, once again, to stagger through the labyrinth.

"Don't move, Anne, just don't move. I'm coming back for you as soon as I take out Central. No one's ever gotten this far, this might be the last chance. It's become too smart, it knows our ways now. I have to do this. I'm almost there."

He would need to find the medicine quickly. Besides the cut to his side, he sensed extreme exhaustion welling up deep inside him. Strange... he used to enjoy this type of feeling after a close race back in training, the feeling of giving all and collapsing in triumph. Each step now required a colossal effort. Derek drove on, the image of reaching the expected medicine the only thing keeping him upright. *Find the medicine first, and then take out the central computer.* According to the map, the access point to the mainframe was only a few doors beyond his present location. Reassured by the weight of the cluster bomb in his backup, he paused at the doorway, drawing all of his energy into a single effort to push beyond the blinding fatigue and enter the room.

An inky darkness greeted him. Though he could see nothing, he sensed that something was horribly wrong. Derek searched the blackness in vain for a cabinet, a med pack, anything to relieve the utter exhaustion. *The room setup is different than the map, but how is this possible? Trusted souls had lost their lives in stitching* together images of the inner hallways of central's defense. Something alien, an awful presence, was here with him. An unnatural, sickly sweet smell of polished metal burned his nostrils, forcing him to collapse to the floor, completely draining him of the last of his energy. Derek knew that he was dying.

"Welcome." The voice was devoid of any emotion.

Overhead, a small pinpoint of light appeared and began to spread outward. A globe of light encircled the room, illuminating it. *Bare, no cabinets. Nothing at all of use.* Derek realized the map was a trick, the mission a lie. Someone, or something, had set him up to fail.

The voice continued, its strength increased by the size of the globe, but still utterly lacking in feeling. "The screen at the top should be of interest to you."

Barely able to lift up his head, Derek watched in horror as Anne's motionless body filled the screen. As the camera panned backwards, the scene incorporated several robed figures, all moving silently away from Anne. *Guardians.*

"Rebels are not tolerated. Justice is fair and swift. This is as it has always been, and always will be." Behind Derek robed figures gathered. As they moved into the room, they formed a circle around him.

Chapter One

Nic hated the move.

When his mom initially approached him about her job transfer, his first thoughts were that it might not be such a bad thing. He had always heard living near the coast had its perks. *I can see beaches, plenty of sun... maybe the chance to meet girls.* Tommy said he would come and visit sometimes, and Tommy's usually disapproving parents gave their consent, surprising even Nic. So, if his one and only friend was planning to visit, at least seasonally, and Tommy's parents were willing to pay for it... well, he found himself, over the last few months, almost looking forward to the move.

Not anymore. The original lure of the change in location wore off quickly in the first few weeks as Nic found himself feeling alone. His mom was always at work, the requirements at her new job forced her to stay late every night. Pizza had become stale; even his favorite, pineapple and mushrooms, he now detested.

Worst of all were the things he now missed, which he hadn't realized were so important. Back home, after his dad disappeared, the places they had gone together grew exponentially in importance. In the first few months, walks by the pool where his dad taught him to swim and the field where he had learned to ride a bike brought painful waves of memories. As time passed, fear replaced sorrow, as Nic realized his dad might not come back. Acceptance finally arrived, giving him the opportunity to visit these places when he struggled with his performance at school or had a fight with his mom; imagining that his dad was walking with him, giving him advice.

He hadn't thought about those walks for a few years; working part-time after school to help support his mom didn't allow for time to revisit. Yet those places were never far away, either beyond the woods or behind the government buildings, depending on whether he was at school or work. Now that he was nearly a thousand miles across the country, the distance seemed immense.

Nic pulled himself out of his unhappy thoughts and headed up the steps. Ronald Reagan High School was an old, large structure, the lack of any grav-lifts to the higher floors as testament to its age. *Anything is better than staying at home these last few weeks, though.* He had come to consider his home a prison rather than the ideal summer vacation spot he thought it would be.

Students watched him as he made his way to his homeroom, sizing him up along the way. *Faces might be different, but types are still the same. Those three in the corner, trying to break into the hallway's environmental access panel—Hackers. The beefy guy at his locker with the swarm of holo-medals pinned to his varsity jacket, each replaying his final match victories— the State Champion. And of course, the Smart Kids who took classes over the summer at the nearby State University already have their mini-Screens out comparing the results of yesterday's final exams.* Other than these, the nameless rabble, the great majority who seemed to drift by unnoticed from year to year, they were there too. All looked up as he went by, taking account of him for a second before moving to their own homerooms.

Nic entered his class and found an empty seat. The top of the seat seemed to be splitting, but was still useable. He gazed around the room, making comparisons with last year's classroom back east. Here, the desks had mini-Screen outlets that would allow access to the school's mainframe. They were old. His previous school had universal outlets which could accommodate any mini-Screen; here he would have to search for an outlet for his mini-Screen. *The back of the room has only one 3D holographic chamber and the enviro discs look old. I remember this back in 6th grade. When are they going to upgrade?*

Sighing with disappointment, he turned back to his desk, and realized something was wrong. *Where's my chair?* He looked around at the other students; they had been there, already in their seats, except for one student at the desk immediately in front of his. This rather large individual had come in and taken the chair while Nic had his back turned. The split at the top of the chair confirmed it.

Summoning up the courage to face the gargantuan, Nic approached him. "Excuse me, that's my chair." The room fell silent. Nic tapped him lightly on the back to get his attention.

Immediately, the boy rose, dwarfing Nic by more than a foot. It was not only the height, but the size that made him realize this was the same kid out in the hallway with the medals. All of the others were watching intently. The hulk brought his face down close to Nic's face, reminding him of a giant bear closing in on its prey. "Don't touch me, if you know what is good for you," he whispered, ending with a sharp poke from a sausage-sized finger to Nic's left shoulder.

Feeling angry and embarrassed, Nic momentarily dismissed his precarious situation and attempted to take back what was rightfully his.

"Get lost," the monster barked, as he removed the chair from Nic's grasp and held it high over his head. "Nobody cares about you, little new boy."

Just great. I sure am going to like it here.

Later in the cafeteria, Nic sat alone. His soy patty from the vending machine wasn't very appealing, but he wasn't much in the mood for any kind of food at the moment, anyway. "This is what it's like, being the new kid," he muttered to himself. "Not much fun."

Nic was certain he felt eyes boring down on him from behind, but when he turned around, all the other students were talking amongst themselves. He almost wished someone were glaring at him, at least that would acknowledge his presence. *I can't believe Tommy is due in two months; that's sixty days, 1,440 hours, somewhere around 80,000 minutes.* Nic found himself growing more depressed the more he calculated.

Feeling again that someone was looking at him, Nic looked up and was rewarded with a smile. A boy roughly Nic's height was looking down at him. "Mind if I join you?" the newcomer asked.

"No, no, go right ahead," Nic blurted in response, hoping he didn't sound too eager for company.

"Thanks." The boy set his tray down, pulled over a chair which squeaked slightly as he ran it across the floor, and sat. "Don't worry about Beast," the boy began. "Yes, I was there, in homeroom with you. That's what we all call him, not to his face of course. No one wants a pounding. You think the name fits?"

Nic recalled the angry, sweaty face looming close, but this time the image made him laugh. "Beast, yeah, I like it. That's original. Did you make it up?"

The other boy chuckled, and then shook his head. "No, wish I could take credit for that one, but my friend Bobby came up with it. 'Bout a year ago, right after Jake, that's the Beast's real name, pushed my head into a toilet."

"Ouch. Always wondered what that would feel like. Managed to avoid it somehow."

"Well, I can tell you it's pretty awful. Especially if, you know, something is already in there."

"Oh man," Nic responded. He tried to feel bad for him, but the image of this boy screaming and kicking as his head met the dirty water caused him to laugh. "Sorry."

"That's okay," the boy replied. "It is kind of funny, looking back. I was worried I would have to go back to class smelling like pee, but no one noticed."

The two fell silent, wondering what they could possibly talk about next. After a few moments, the other boy began again. "Name's Conner." As he smiled again, he extended his right hand. "And you are?"

"Nic. Good to meet you Conner."

"Likewise. And what brings you to these sacred halls of learning, Nic?"

"Job transfer. My mom. Got here about two months ago."

"Uh huh," Connor replied thoughtfully. "Been there, done that. A few years ago, my dad and me. Ever since, I have been privileged to serve as an esteemed student at this highly respected campus. Hey, who's kidding? This place sucks."

"Great, I have a lot to look forward to then."

Conner considered this for a few seconds, hoping he wouldn't scare off this new student. "I make it sound worse than it is. There are those like the Beast, just stay clear of them. He is only establishing his territory with you. Hey, tomorrow I'll introduce you to some of my friends. It's really okay here."

A faint chime sounded overhead, ending the lunch hour. Slowly, the students gathered their belongings and methodically headed out the door. "Just like cattle, off you go to the slaughter," Conner smirked.

"What, what was that?"

"Nothing important Nic, a term I read once in a history book, I think. Anyway, off to class. See ya."

"Yeah, bye."

For the third time in the day, Nic felt someone watching him. He searched the room, but it was empty. As he exited, he didn't notice a girl standing behind the vending machine, watching him closely.

Later that day, Nic returned home. After surfing through several thousand channels, chat and game sites, he still hadn't found anything remotely interesting on the Screen. His mom had scolded him over the last few weeks as he would sit listlessly on the couch, pressing the button, over and over, cycling though list after list of the vast types of entertainment available to download. "Nic, cut it out. You're wasting so much time," his mom would scold. "By now you could have created your own site." Knowing that he would find nothing of interest, he still went through the mechanical motion of checking the Screen, channel after channel, site after site. The process became a daily ritual, a reminder of how unhappy he was. As always, he finally grew bored and turned the machine off.

He picked up his mini-Screen, not expecting much to be different, but feeling too lethargic to move. The ongoing investigation back east, in New York, regarding the first computer-controlled automobile crash in fifty years captured the attention of the nation, leading to speculation that the continual rise in seawater levels, which had been submerging parts of the city over the last ten years, had finally inundated one of the traffic control centers, thus leading to the crash. The upcoming trip to Europa to validate initial findings suggesting the existence of microbial life was also causing widespread interest, though a number of people were also finding the idea unsettling.

Nic paused for a few seconds to read a few of the introductory sentences about *Movie Star 2.0,* the sequel to the original hit where you could script, and even take the leading role, in your own homemade movie. Nothing held his interest for long though, and he sighed as he shifted on the living room couch, tossed his mini-Screen, and looked out the window. *There's nothing of interest to me anymore. I just want to go back home. To my real home.*

Nic Rocke   Marc Sherrod

Chapter Two

Nic awoke with a start. He realized he must have been asleep when the front door chimed. Glancing at the wall, he saw that it was already late, well past the time he needed to have addressed his homework. "Great," he said quietly. "Mom won't be happy again."

Trying to get to his room unnoticed would be impossible. Mom's path coming up the stairs would cut right across his. *Besides, it's time to tell Mom how unhappy I am.*

Her pattern was highly predictable. Once in the kitchen, she would drop her bags, all except the one containing her uniform, which she would hang with care in the laundry. The clinking of the hanger against the rail in the closet confirmed that she was right on time. Nic never asked her why she didn't recycle her uniform daily in the nano-bin outside the apartment complex where thousands of microscopic machines would set to work removing stains and repairing any tearing the uniform might have experienced at the factory. He knew she couldn't afford it; they couldn't afford it. Occasionally, in the middle of the night, he would find Mom cleaning and knitting the uniform herself. Nic marveled at her resourcefulness as it was difficult to find the thread and needles required to do the work.

Usually after setting the uniform in place, his mother would come into the living room, take a seat on the couch, and stare at the wall for a few minutes. He wondered what must go through her mind at such times. *Maybe she regretted the move out here?*

The day must have been unusually hard, for she didn't immediately come into the living room. *The shift manager is probably punishing her again.* Repairing the bots on the assembly line was grueling work, and not meeting quota had dire consequences. Nic knew from the brief descriptions Mom sometimes gave that all it took was one unusual action on the part of a bot to bring attention to it, sometimes to the point where a shift manager would order a full deconstruction and follow-up investigation. Occasionally, Mom's team would have two bots to investigate on a shift which would hold up the entire assembly line. *I don't understand why they just don't make better bots in the first place, like in China.*

Not wanting to make things worse, Nic stealthily approached the door to the kitchen and looked in. There at the counter, was the slumped form of his mom, her head buried in her hands. The occasional shudder let him known that she was sobbing, crying softly into her arms in order to avoid waking him. Nic felt a stabbing guilt burn through him as he realized how difficult this move must be for her, as well. For now, he would need to fight his problems by himself. Carefully, he crept past the kitchen and headed to his room.

****

Over the next several days Conner kept his word. He introduced Nic to several of the boys in homeroom, who all had one thing in common, a severe dislike for the Beast. At one point or another, they had all been his victims. Conner had the distinct privilege of having received the Beast's undivided attention in the bathroom, as he had mentioned earlier to Nic. Michael had been beaten up outside near the gym, and Bobby's plasti-I.D. card had been stolen near the front entrance to the school. When Conner told Nic about who he was about to meet, and their unfortunate encounters, Nic assumed all the boys were small, weak kids who were the perfect material for bullies to target. Yet this was not the case. If anything, it seemed the Beast did not discriminate. He picked on everyone.

Michael was rather athletic, one of the better players on the school's hover-soccer team. His speed allowed for him to strike quickly from midfield, using the springs in his shoes to propel himself over the opposition and receive the ball just in time for a shot past the goalie. Bobby was slightly shorter than Michael, and enjoyed quieter hobbies, such as programming his home studio with the latest downloadable games. At twenty-five exabytes his studio capacity was the envy of his friends, who used every excuse to get out of homework to spend more time at Bobby's house playing the scenarios he had modified.

Conner had meant well to help Nic adjust to his school, but despite all of the introductions, Nic still felt very alone. The boys had their own friendship circles, and from what he remembered, when new kids showed up at his school back east, it took them a while to be accepted. In the meantime, he would have to endure the loneliness; a slow ache left him feeling hollow inside. Even the occasional grimace from the Beast was welcome, as it acknowledged his presence within the vastness of the school.

On the Wednesday before the Thanksgetting holiday, where families typically gorged themselves on food and spent the rest of the day huddled around the Screen surfing channels, at lunch Nic once again felt the stare on his back he had experienced a dozen times. He'd thought on several occasions to tell Conner, but he wasn't sure what Connor would think. Conner was not yet a friend, more like a person with whom he was on friendly terms. Telling him about strange feelings of someone's eyes on his back might just drive him away, forcing Nic to start all over in trying to make friends. Nic looked around, trying to find the source of the staring, but as always, came up empty-handed.

"It's Willow," Conner casually remarked.

"What?"

"Willow, she's the one that's been starting at you. I guess a few weeks now, maybe more. Back there, third column on the right." Nic turned around and focused, but still saw nothing. "She saw you turning and scrambled," Conner continued.

Willow. The small girl with the short blonde hair who sat at the back of the classroom and talked to no one. He knew her, or to be more precise, knew her name, but really nothing else. Nic thought this incredible. If this had been going on all this time, why did Conner not mention anything?

"So she's been there a while watching me, and you knew it?" Nic exhaled, trying to keep from getting frustrated.

"Yep, but it is nothing unusual. She's been that way with new people ever since I can remember."

Nic considered this. *A girl's paying attention to me. This has never happened before.* A rushing swell of excitement flushed his face, apparently obvious to Conner.

"Don't get too excited there, Romeo. She's a weird one, not the kind you want following you around."

"Why, what did she do?"

Conner remained silent for a few minutes. "It's not exactly what she did but... well, what happened to her. Both of her parents died several years ago."

For the remainder of the day, Nic couldn't get Willow out of his mind. His dad's disappearance had always haunted Nic, but at the bottom of his despair was the hope that one day he would meet him, somehow, again. For Willow to know this could never happen with both of her parents must be unbearable.

****

The next day in homeroom, the students were directed by the Central Computer Instructor to work in pairs. As usual, with this type of project, students who had scored similar interests on the standardized tests were selected to work with each other in order to maximize productivity. The CCI further explained in its unwavering, mechanical voice, that the students were to pick out a scientific event of historical significance and present to the class in a week's time. As Nic approached the Screen, his name and his partner's appeared.

"Nic R.—Willow S." The girl looked in his direction, and smiled faintly. *It seems the CCI thinks she and I have something in common.*

Over the next few days Nic became hopeful. Several times in the hallways at school Michael and Bobby would look his way and acknowledge his presence with a slight dip of the head. While this was not a full-blown greeting, it was a start.

Nic found that he spent more and more of his time thinking about Willow. The girl was a mystery, and something of a tragedy, too. She no longer stood behind the columns at school staring at him, but on occasion in the classroom, he caught her glance. Willow would quickly look away whenever that happened.

During his first assignment of the year with the 3D Holographic Chamber, Nic didn't see Willow coming out of the little room when he bumped into her and knocked her down. He chided himself for being in such a hurry and offered to help the girl pick up her Enviro discs; but Willow scrambled away and retreated to one of the corners of the classroom.

The Beast was watching and let out an evil, mocking laugh. Being in no mood for the antics of this monster, Nic returned his gaze with his own look of hate. It was from that point the hostility between the two went from bad to horrible.

Had he not been preoccupied with rethinking again and again the embarrassing act of knocking Willow down, Nic might have seen the attack coming on his walk home from school. The crashing pain to his right eye awoke him from his thoughts and he turned to face whatever had smashed into him. Through blurred vision he could make out the hulking form of the Beast and the two smaller forms of his toadies clinging to either side of him. The younger boys were letting out shrieks of victory at the sucker punch and congratulated the giant by clapping him on the shoulders. "Don't you ever make that face again, loser," the Beast snapped. "Learn your place. Next time I'll take your whole head off."

Even after a few minutes, Nic could still hear the three of them far down the road reliving the moment, the story growing more fantastic with each telling. "I was going to hit him, but you already hit him good," one of the toadies called out.

"Going soft on me, eh? You want to get hit too?" the Beast replied. An eerie silence followed. With a swollen eye and ringing in his head, Nic managed to stand and continue back towards the apartment.

Nic Rocke

Marc Sherrod

Chapter Three

"You're right, it is old," Conner said. "Not to be rude, but it's kind of like everything in your apartment here, Nic. Haven't seen buttons like this in a couple of years. What do you think, Bobby?"

Startled, Bobby looked up from playing with his mini-Screen and looked towards Connor. Slowly he sighed, lifted his hefty frame and ponderously made his way over to where the other boys had gathered around the home medical unit. "Definitely, definitely old," Bobby, replied, and resumed surfing.

"That's it, nothing else?" Nic asked. "I thought by having you guys over you could help me with this thing. And my eye."

With a look of disdain, Bobby turned his mini-Screen off and looked towards Conner. "Please inform our new friend here that my time is precious. The less time I spend researching our new adventure, the less time any of you will have playing it over at my place. I'm trying to figure out a way to make this download happen without paying for it. Worked once, remember last year? Then they found out, thanks to you," he pointed at Michael; "so next time, don't say anything at school to anybody. You all think I'm crazy, but it's true, everything said there gets reported. Froze my credits and I got kicked off the server."

Michael tried to stifle a laugh but failed and started coughing, earning a sharp glance from Bobby.

"Okay everyone, let's stay focused, alright? Really, I can't take you two anywhere without you making a scene," Conner said, rolling his eyes in disbelief. "You did ask for our help Nic, and indeed we will help you."

Nic, Conner and Michael resumed looking at the home medical unit while Bobby continued to find a way to make the illegal game download. The device was dirtied and several of the switches were worn with use, but otherwise it was intact. "You and your mom definitely need to upgrade this, Nic," Conner suggested. "You might not be able to download directly. Having a service bot come out to check this though isn't cheap. Anyway, let's take a look at that eye."

After flipping the master switch, the device began to stir to life. A slow crackling noise even caught Bobby's attention, but it soon subsided. Nic thought he saw a tiny drift of smoke pass out of the back of the unit, but convinced himself his impaired vision was making him see things. Once the machine settled down and a soothing hum emerged, the boys resumed.

"The layout is different than ours, but some of the labeling is the same. Virtual Doctor Call, see it, over there on the right? That's what we need," Conner concluded.

The screen on the wall in front of the device flickered several times before a middle-aged man appeared, smiling faintly with alert eyes staring out towards them. It was clear to the boys the holographic image represented a doctor.

"Haven't seen that hairstyle in a while," Nic began. "Clothes look like they are made of real cotton. It really is old. Sure this things works?"

"Yeah, it will work," Michael replied. "My grandparents had an ancient one, first model I think, right after the war. They kept it in good shape."

"Quiet," Conner snapped. "Gotta think what to say to this holo." After a few moments he addressed the virtual doctor. "See, my friend here has a swollen eye. We aren't sure what to do."

The virtual image seemed to peer directly at Nic, sending a shiver through the boy. Most images were not this lifelike, certainly not holos this old. *Perhaps it is meant to make anyone feel as if they are talking to a real doctor.* The image responded with a pleasant but professional voice. "Please take the scanner located at the side of the medical unit and place it directly in front of the area affected."

"Go ahead, Nic, it's over there," Michael pointed out.

"I don't know. Doesn't look like it has been used for a long time. Sure it won't make it worse?" Nic asked.

"No, these things are pretty safe. That scanner will run a test and tell the computer what it finds. Don't worry, it's not going to poke your eye out," Conner reassured his friend.

With a look of doubt, Nic slowly brought the scanner up. The handheld resembled an old style game controller his great grandparents would have used back in the early days of virtual gaming. Video games, they used to call them. Nic remembered trying one in a museum. They weren't much fun, all you did was stare at a screen and press a few buttons.

"Excellent," the doctor continued. "To proceed, locate the scanning plate and place it opposite the affected area, one inch above the surface. When ready, depress the red button at the back of the device. You will notice a tingling sensation to the affected area. This is natural, an integral stage of the diagnosis process." Wincing slightly, as if expecting the device to remove his eyeball, Nic did as instructed. A warm, flooding feeling moved slowly clockwise around his eye, but stopped after a few moments. The screen then divided in half. The doctor appeared on the left, while words and phrases flowed down from the top of the right side of the screen. Nic wondered what a Nasolacriminal Duct was and if the words "damage" and "periorbital hematoma" appearing in the same sentence was a bad thing. The words continued to scroll. Nic had no idea the eye was so complex. After a few minutes, he began to understand that items listed in green were areas of his eye left unaffected, but items listed in red appeared to suffer from trauma, abrasion or hemorrhaging. *At least I can still see.*

After a few more moments, the scrolling stopped. "I'm impressed," Bobby blurted out from the back of the room. The others were surprised their friend was paying attention. "See how the doctor's head moves as if considering each new line of reported information. Even blinks and sighs occasionally. Early prototype for what we have now."

From the side of the machine, a slot opened and a small bottle popped out. Nic picked it up and peered into it. A viscous while fluid was inside. The doctor then issued instructions. "Apply twice daily, once in the morning and once at night. If the condition persists after three days, return to this unit for further medical attention."

Nic looked from the doctor to the right side of the screen. He couldn't believe that all of the phrases highlighted in red meant that a small bottle of creamy goo would help him. Nic decided it was best to ask questions now. "Excuse me, not that I doubt you, but all that stuff to the right. Those words, sentences; Hema, hema, whatever it's called. What does all that mean?"

As before, the doctor began to nod as if deeply considering the information, this time in the form of a question, then responded. "Potential answers are beyond the means of understanding given the subject's current level of education. The subject is directed to inquire through the Screen or through local library resources for content meaning. If there are no further medical needs, this program session will terminate." To which it promptly turned off after ten seconds, detecting no further inquiries.

"You've got to be kidding," Conner said. "How insulting."

"Wow Nic, I think it just called you stupid," Bobby laughed. "Primitive technology but must have had a great programmer. Kind of like me." Bobby looked down at his mini-Screen in disgust. "Stupid download, still not done."

Is the day going to get any worse? Now even a computer is making fun of me, Nic thought.

Nic Rocke

Marc Sherrod

Chapter Four

       At first he drew looks from students and staff alike as they paused in their daily lives to consider Nic's new appearance. The shiner seemed to grow darker and larger by the day. As it became common knowledge that the Beast once again was the source of someone's pain, the black eye became part of the daily routine. No one was surprised when the admin bot visited the classroom to pull the Beast out again for a meeting with the principal, this time to discuss Nic's injury.

       Lunch had become part of the boring, daily ritual. Nic often wouldn't even be able to recall what he had ordered the day before. Drab, gray and tasteless described most of the menu. He sometimes wondered what made up the food and decided it was best not to know. At his previous school the food was not much better. Years ago, Nic had heard the standardized national lunch menu for all schools was a result of once curbing the obesity crisis; at one time, eighty percent of the population fell into this category. Mitigating the heart diseases of the time became a national obsession. Supposedly, the food was extremely healthy now, but no one wanted to eat it.

Gross stuff. I better eat it though, or my stomach is going to growl through the test later in the day. He noticed, as he was waiting in line for the kitchen bots to serve him the unappetizing gruel, Willow sitting alone at one of the tables. Nic looked over at his friends' table where Michael was animatedly describing something to the others. From the look of it, Nic guessed that it was probably about last week's hover-soccer victory against the hated rival from the other side of the city.

He looked back at the wilting form of Willow, barely making out her unmoving eyes under the blond tangles of hair. Someone else was also obviously unimpressed with today's meal, as the lumps of overcooked matter lay untouched in front of her. Given that they were to be project partners, Nic decided it was time to approach the girl. *I better not scare her. Maybe I should walk directly to her where she can see me coming.*

Once within sight, it was clear to Willow her new partner's intentions. Her eyes grew large and panicky, shifting first left, and then right. She felt frozen under his gaze, unable to move. She swallowed hard and felt her heart racing. Nic was sure he heard a mousy squeak from the girl as he came to a halt in front of her.

"Hi, uh, partner," Nic began, regretting at once the too informal tone of his greeting. *Whoever called someone that?* He dismissed quickly a recollection of old movies from the previous century his grandparents used to watch with him late at night, where all the cowboys used that greeting.

A bead of sweat would form a river over his injured eye if he didn't act soon. Having the black eye was bad enough, having it look like a soupy, dark lake would be beyond embarrassment.

Pushing through an uncomfortable feeling of panic, he sat down quickly. Willow focused her gaze on the food in front of her, saying nothing. The enormous size of her eyes, however, gave Nic the impression of a caged animal too scared to move. The idea that he was the predator in her thoughts momentarily stung him, and he realized if he didn't win her over now, he never would. He decided to try the comical approach first.

"Yeah, I see you like the food here, too. Hey, I have an idea. We could use this as our focus for our project. Maybe we could call it 'Cafeteria Catastrophe: Forty Years of Student Suffering.'"

Willow remained silent, unmoving. After a few seconds, there was still no response. "Okay, bad idea. You're right. We should take this a little more seriously. I never have really had a chance to talk to you in class. I don't know your interests, your hobbies. Maybe we could start there?" Again, no response. Willow's eyes seemed to dim a little and grow smaller. Her eyes still remained targeted on the few feet in front of her. Nic felt he was losing the battle but decided to try once more. "Look, um, I'm not really good at this. Being new here, I'm still learning about this place. I heard, well, I heard about what happened to you last year. My dad left when I was young, I don't know where he went. There are different stories, but I really don't know for sure. Anyway, sorry what happened to you, Willow."

Nic was certain a soft sigh escaped from the girl. Her eyes remained fixed, but began filling with tears. She remained in place. Nic decided he wouldn't be able to get through to this girl. "Gotta go. Bye Willow. See you later in class." As he stood to throw the rest of his lunch into the nano-disposal unit, he heard the girl speak for the first time.

"Nic?"

"Yeah?" he turned around to face the girl.

"Thanks."

Chapter Five

"So what kind of Hist-science project are you interested in, Nic?" Willow asked as she sipped her Fibro-B.

Nic looked at the ceiling, trying to come up with something. "Not sure. Maybe we can look to see what's happened over the last thirty years or so."

Willow paused, lost in thought for a few moments, and then started to rise. "Good idea. I've got something just for it. Hang on."

The girl disappeared around one of the corners in her parents' library. Nic wondered how Willow managed to live here alone. He heard the virtual counselor at school had determined it would be best for her to remain living at this location despite what had happened. He didn't agree, but shrugged off the idea. *If an old medical program thought I'm stupid, what do I know about modern counseling?*

Nic heard cabinets open and close, a sound of ruffling, and finally a squeal of triumph from Willow. Apparently she had found something important. Willow soon returned with a heavy, old book. She blew the dust off the cover, causing Nic to choke. "Sorry, it's been a while since anyone looked at this. I remember when I was young and Dad would have me on his lap reading this with me. It's from a long time ago. Not sure exactly when."

Willow handed the volume over to him. Nic eagerly grasped it with both hands. He found it odd that the girl with the reputation of being a loner was so willingly engaging. *Perhaps she just never had a chance to feel like she could really talk to someone.* He knew the feeling well.

"So this is a book?" he asked excitedly, opening the cover and staring at the title page. As Nic received the tome, he was surprised at its weight. It was much heavier than he anticipated. He imagined a person trying to carry around a thousand of these in the old days in a large bag, just as he could carry thousands or more virtual books on his mini-Screen. The idea was comical, yet the more he thought of it, the more he envied the people of the past holding books, reading them, and passing them to friends. With the book came a solid feeling that you actually held a valuable possession, that it was your own. Slowly, he leafed through the volume, pouring over the faded pictures. Willow smiled as Nic closed the cover and stared thoughtfully out the window.

"I reacted the same way when I read one myself for the first time," Willow reminisced. "Couldn't put it down. My parents used to have lots of them, before... well... you know."

Nic brought his gaze to focus on the girl, a look of compassion crossing his face. "I'm sorry, we don't have to do this if it brings back painful memories. We can go on the Screen instead."

"No, it's fine." Willow breathed in deep, bit her lower lip, and straightened. "I want to do this. I think it's important we do this project using this book."

Taking the book back and opening to one of the chapters, Willow read aloud. *"Expectations in the advancement of medical sciences, 2025 and beyond; Early challenges in the development of an artificial pancreas; DNA research in the advancement of depression intervention; in-vitro meat experimentation...* the list goes on. Wait, that last one. In-vitro meat?" Willow looked up at Nic, puzzlement clear on her face.

Nic tried to recall the expression. He'd heard it before, reference to artificial meat of one type or another. Technically, all meat was artificial now, as was just about all food. Nobody now thought of it as a bad thing, but he imagined the first generation of people dealing with this novel concept, and as a result, their lives changing immensely. He knew the explanation would make Willow queasy.

"Yeah, I think I remember a little bit about it now," Nic began. Delicately, he couched his words. "Back then they began experimenting with food, I think in an attempt to be able to feed everybody. That was before countries enforced limits on the populations after the war." Nic paused, finding no way around the truth. "It used to be that people would eat real meat... you know... animals."

An expression of amazement passed by Willow's face, and then one of doubt. The girl broke out into giggles, punching playfully his arm. "Good one, Nic," she smirked, her expression however turning stone cold as she realized he was telling the truth. All she could utter was a single word. "Barf."

"What?" Nic responded, unsure of her meaning. "What did you just say?"

Composing herself, Willow continued. "Since we are talking about a long time ago, I thought I would use one of their expressions. It meant... well... something between 'I don't believe it' and 'I feel sick from thinking about it'. Anyway, why don't we continue, we have to be able to find something of interest in there."

"Here, let me take a look, maybe from another part of it. Let's see, *Advances in computer technology; Moore's Law holds through 2055, when nano-built carbon filaments make it possible for much more rapid advancement in computer speed*. Let's keep going. *Voice synthesis; holographic projection; home defense and climate control systems*. Look at these pictures, Willow. Grandma had one of these."

Turning the book in his friend's direction, they both enjoyed a hearty laugh. The picture displayed a young woman in her thirties, dressed in the clothing of the time, a single, satin outfit complete with the short-cropped hairstyle. The Xenon 750 home computer grid promised to keep all rooms at the individual lighting and temperature preference settings, create all meals and alert all inhabitants of unexpected guests approaching the home.

"Maybe we should just leave this one in the past," Willow concluded. "Keep going."

"It says here universities made exponential leaps in the field of artificial intelligence," Nic said. "In 2030, first two on the west coast, then one in London, and finally a fourth in Shanghai all claimed to have created a computer more intelligent than man." Nic paused and placed the book down carefully, treating it as a prized possession. He tried to search his memory. There was an element of familiarity to the term, 'artificial intelligence,' but he was unable to place it.

"I remember this one," Willow mentioned proudly. "Back then, the goal was to see if computers could outthink a human being. At first, they played games with the computers, who would win because they wouldn't get tired from all the games, while the humans required rest. Eventually, they tried to build into the computers a sense of morals, but they always failed. The logical choices were not always in the best interests of people. One time, one of the computers was asked to make a choice between a few horses and a single human in a survival situation. The computer chose the horses. When asked, the answer was that the horses would survive longer in the winter conditions than the man, and thus were more useful. I heard that one when I was a little kid. Something my parents told me."

"I'm impressed," Nic said. "You certainly have a memory."

"Thanks Nic," Willow responded.

"You know, I think we have our Hist-science project. With your ability to recall these kinds of details, we are sure to get a good score. Besides, I would like to find out why the early computers couldn't make the right moral choices."

Nic Rocke Marc Sherrod

Chapter Six

Initially, Nic met Tommy's call last night with great enthusiasm, eager to forget the fact that Tommy had not returned several of his calls over the last week. Nic needed his friend now more than ever before with the recent humiliation at school from the Beast. At first, he had wondered if Tommy's Screen was broken, as that had happened once before, about three years ago. They had both laughed at that incident as it forced Tommy to come all the way over to his house to talk to Nic. *It was like something out of the Stone Age. He had to visit my house instead of using the Screen.*

Last night's call was strange, and it bothered Nic that he was unable to determine exactly why. Tommy seemed distant, almost like a stranger. They joked a few times about some of the other kids at the school back east, but after that, there wasn't much to say. Tommy had outgrown the hover-bike Nic had given him several birthdays ago. The vehicle had become a "hand-me-down" to his happy little sister who had somehow managed not to knock down anyone on her first day of trying out the unexpected gift. His friend nodded as Nic recounted his first few days at the new school, and actually showed interest at the retelling of Willow's mysterious gazing from behind barriers and the visit to her home.

The conversation ended abruptly, as it seemed someone else was trying to call Tommy on the Screen. In the past, Tommy wouldn't have bothered to answer the other call, but it was clear to Nic that Tommy wanted to go. He promised that once the call was over he would get back to Nic, but he never did. And that was yesterday.

****

Nic was tempted to call Willow on his mini-Screen and tell her not to bother to come to the research center. The drizzle added to Nic's already downtrodden mood. He considered going inside the center first and then waiting for Willow there, but the other kids in his class might see him alone, and he was concerned about what they might think. *Poor new kid, still all alone.* The last thing he needed, and wanted, was someone's pity.

As he activated his mini-Screen and input Willow's contact, he noticed a rain-soaked figure emerge from behind the research center and start heading towards the main entrance. *People are more likely to pity her than me, just look at her.* As he started towards the entrance, he noticed the figure answer her mini-Screen. Nic instantly knew the figure in front of him was Willow.

"Hello," the voice trembled with cold.

Nic stumbled for a minute. "Hi, uh Willow? Just wondering where you're at."

"Almost there. Should be inside in a few minutes. I will meet you just inside the front entrance."

"I'll be there in a few minutes, too. See you soon." *Of course. Willow would have walked to the center, given no one was available to drop her off. It must have been a mile for her. It is only a few blocks for me.* Nic could have kicked himself.

The lobby to the research center was massive, as well as ornately decorated. Like most of the other government buildings, the center was old, yet from the interior one wouldn't have been able to notice its age with all of the holographic chambers and other rooms.

Everyone had access to any of the databases, resulting in kids, teenagers, parents and working professionals using the center's resources to pursue their interests and work. When he was little, one of Nic's CCI bots once explained that the centers were set up across the country to provide complete openness to any citizen, the idea being that transparency results in a better informed and less skeptical society. As a kid though, he felt there must have been people out there who had secrets and would not have wanted to share them. As an example, he had never told his mom the truth regarding the smashed window, and the ball he quickly disposed of soon after the break. As the teacher had told him though, fewer secrets were for the better; and like the other kids, he believed its words and had forgotten his doubts.

Willow was waiting near one of the interior doors. She stood shuddering. Her wet hair trickled down, partially covering her eyes. As Nic approached, she smiled gently and tried to stop moving. "Hi, nice day, huh?" she managed, through chattering teeth.

To Nic, Willow seemed absolutely miserable. "Let's get you inside," he began. "Here, this might help." Nic took off his jacket, then his sweatshirt. He still had a t-shirt on underneath, which was no match for the cold sliding though the old doorways. Quickly, he donned his jacket and held his sweatshirt out to Willow.

At first she was unsure what to do with it, but then realized his intention. After putting it on, it was almost comical the way the cuffs engulfed Willow's slight wrists. Her hands were nowhere to be seen. The edge also extended well below her waist, halfway to her knees. Yet she seemed appreciative, and her lips had returned to their normal color. She was no longer shuddering. "Thank you Nic," she whispered. As they headed into the center, Nic felt his face grow hot watching Willow before him, wearing his sweatshirt.

Inside the center, the two of them felt lost. Rows and columns of rooms reached into the distance. Nic didn't realize how far into the ground the center extended, but from this vantage, he was unable to see the bottom. A number of the rooms within sight were occupied; privacy was critical in keeping the integrity of the research center high among the patrons. In one of the rooms, a family was asking questions of the mainframe. Perhaps the parents were helping one of their kids with a homework assignment, as the daughter seemed animated in describing something while the father nodded approvingly. In another location, just off to the left and above, the doors were shut, indicating that the occupant had engaged the holographic mode and was accessing information visually. Nic enjoyed this feature. The best way he had learned about Abraham Lincoln was to stand beside him during the Gettysburg address and hear the famous speech given several centuries ago. His mom hadn't let him enable the interactive feature as she believed the experience would be too intense for his young age. Only two years ago he had relived the Gettysburg experience with the interactive feature engaged and had an incredible adventure.

"Welcome," a monotone voice addressed them. "I am your Cyber Guide to the research center. Mini-Screens please." Both Nic and Willow automatically showed their mini-Screens to the rail above, something they had been trained to do long ago. A globe traveled along the rail system, as did hundreds of others helping other patrons. A pleasant chime, twice, indicated their member-in-good-standing status. "Thank you," the voice continued. "How can I be of service?"

Nic answered, "Well, we wanted to know more about artificial intelligence history." Willow nodded in agreement.

"Certainly," the voice continued. "There is an empty room on this level, five doors down from here. Will you require visual interactivity?"

The two looked at each other, and Willow shook her head. "I don't really like that feature, Nic. Maybe just questions, is that okay?"

"Sure, fine by me." Nic couldn't understand Willow's reluctance as the interactive part was always more exciting. But he let it go.

"Very good. Please follow the illuminated path along the floor. We hope you enjoy the use of these facilities."

Upon entering the room, both of them plugged in their mini-Screens in nearby outlets. A featureless face appeared in the middle of the room, rotating slowly on an axis. The eyes opened, indicating the mainframe was accessible. "Ready," it uttered, in the same monotone voice as the cyber guide.

"We wanted to know about the history of artificial intelligence," Willow asked.

"There are many files under this heading. Please specify parameter particulars."

"We don't have much to go on; maybe we should have brought your book. Do you remember any details?"

"Not really, Nic," Willow responded. "But it's pretty good about giving answers even with a little bit of information. Guess it's worked with a lot of kids over the years." Willow concentrated, and then addressed the face. "This is historical. It involves the question of morality." She looked at Nic with a self-satisfied look on her face and continued. "A computer was once asked about whether a man was more important than a couple of horses. It was winter. Sorry, not much else to go on."

"Checking. Please wait." With voice unwavering, the head continued to rotate slowly.

After a few seconds, it confirmed its findings, once again opening its eyes and coming to a complete stop. "Remote historical archives are accessed. We are sorry for the delay. The event in question was an experiment conducted by one Dr. Stephen Butler, regarded as an expert in the development of artificial intelligence. This was one of several questions posed to several man-made intelligences created at the time..." The face froze in mid-sentence, seeming to counter-rotate momentarily and stop again. Neither Nic nor Willow had ever seen a research center holo behave in this manner. "Apologies. The file... appears... corrupt. Access is no longer maintained. Making note of irregularity for database cataloguing purposes." The face then fell silent.

"That's it?" Nic looked at Willow, her own face puzzled.

"Try again," she urged him.

"We were asking about artificial intelligence. The story of, what did you say, Dr. Butler and the horses. You seemed to shut off."

"Next query please," the holo interrupted.

"I wasn't finished. It was a moral story, he asked a computer about choosing between—"

"Next query. That file, as stated, is not accessible."

Nic stopped, speechless. This had never happened before.

"Weird," was all Willow could say.

Nic Rocke

Chapter Seven

Over the next week, the strange encounter with the holo at the library would find its way into Nic's thoughts. He considered on several occasions to tell his mom, but he concluded that she wouldn't understand. *Mom doesn't have the time to listen to me. She really doesn't understand anyway.* He didn't begrudge her for this, as she was working hard for the two of them to keep this new life. Even if she did sit down for five minutes to listen, from past experience Nic would expect her face to gloss over and her barely moving lips to start recounting the shopping list order she would need to place with the Screen later in the day. *Parents and technology don't mix. I've had to help her so many times with the Screen controls.*

The conversations about the event with Willow at lunch the next day went much better. At first, Conner and the guys didn't know what to do when she started sitting at the edge of their lunch table, occasionally eyeing Nic. Trying to involve her in conversation was impossible, so they generally ignored her. Yet she immediately opened up any time Nic asked her a question, to the point that during a lengthy conversation she would inch closer and closer, almost sitting next to him. The boys eventually lost interest in this surprising turn of events for the extremely shy Willow, as her behavior when discussing things with Nic at the lunch table became routine.

$$****$$

It was a relief for Nic to return to school from the winter holidays. Tommy had decided that going on a trip with one of his classmates instead of coming to see Nic was how he wanted to spend his holiday gift money, putting Nic into one the foulest of moods he had yet to experience since moving across the country.

Life had nearly returned to the "normal" pattern at school of discussions at lunch with friends and angry stares from the Beast, when both Nic and Willow were called to the principal's office. The dreaded admin bot which came to class surprisingly didn't arrive to escort the Beast once again for beating up some unfortunate first-year, but instead calmly slid to Nic's desk and patiently waited. Its luminous, unmoving eyes peered down at him. He wasn't sure how to react as they walked the dreaded path to the main administrative office. The curious gaze of onlookers and Willow's nervous glances were of no comfort to him.

Nic had been to the principal's office just once before. All new students at a high school were required to undergo the less than enjoyable experience of new student orientation, where the few remaining human administrators at an institution babbled about the merits of a school under the watchful supervision of the Monitor, the school's computer link to the outside world. He recalled hearing some years ago that during his parents' educational years, the decision had been made to entrust the running of schools to computers. Supposedly, it was meant to save a lot of money, for who paid computers to do work? Computers also had instantaneous access to massive databases of information, and it was suggested that they also would be the most objective of instructors when it came to developing and grading students. Nic sighed at this last thought, wondering just when it began that parents only seemed to care about grades. As Nic and Willow approached the principal's office, they looked at each other, and then slowly stepped across the imagined, invisible barrier at the doorframe only a few unfortunate students ever faced.

Mr. Thomas, the school principal, was a pudgy, short man who had a tendency to take off his glasses and rub them incessantly with a cloth when nervous. Nic remembered this from his meeting with the principal when he first arrived at the school, and he was not surprised now to see the adult behind a closed door, sweating profusely, obviously engaged in conversation with someone as he stroked his glasses with a worn, stained cloth. The man sighed heavily as he emerged from his office, then straightened and coughed several times as he readied himself to lecture to the two students.

"Come in, children," the principal managed in a high, strained voice. "Please sit down, over there."

Mr. Thomas indicated with a quick wave of his hand the chairs in front of his desk where Nic and Willow were expected to listen to his discourse. Nic found it odd that no one else had been in the room. *Does the principal have the habit of talking to himself?* Nic wondered.

"Wonderful, you are both seated," the adult stated the obvious. "Now, do you have any understanding as to why the two of you are in my office today?" Leaning forward and staring accentuated the principal's timid question, as if the man were trying to draw attention away from himself and focus on the two students.

Warmth surged through Nic's body as he felt placed under a spotlight. Out of the corner of his eye he could see Willow fidgeting, clearly as uncomfortable as he was with this attention. After neither of them responded, the principal launched into his speech.

"You see children," he began, "most visits to my office in recent years are usually by those students who have, how shall I say, corrective issues I need to address. In short, students who have difficulty adjusting to the academic rigor or pace of life in this school at some point arrive here. My job is to work directly with those students with the primary goal of effecting adequate rehabilitation in order for such students to be able to return to their classrooms in a timely fashion. Does this make sense to you?"

The principal paused for effect, letting this final question sink in. Nic could see that the man was trembling slightly, though trying hard to maintain composure. He wasn't sure he was expected to answer the question, and wasn't entirely certain where Mr. Thomas was headed with this. Nic therefore, remained silent.

"Well, I am certainly not in the habit of answering my own questions," the principal continued, "but I can see that you might need some understanding of what all of this means." Mr. Thomas then looked towards the ceiling, as if lost in thought. "Right. Perhaps with the two of you, the direct approach will work best. Last week, you both visited our local library. Do you recall this event?"

Certain that a rhetorical question would not be asked a second time, Nic responded. "Yes sir, I do. Willow and I were trying to finish a project for class and thought it best to do some research at the library."

"Very good, very good Mr. Rocke. It is useful in the rehabilitation process to be truthful, willing, and upfront. This is a good start. Now then, what events proceeded to take place on that day?"

Before Nic could continue, Willow joined in the conversation, eager to add her own thoughts. "You see sir; we thought the library would have the necessary resources for us to do our Hist-science project. It's a bit of a far walk for me, but I didn't want to disappoint Nic, and I haven't been to the library in a while. At least not since when..." Willow trailed off, casting her eyes downward towards the floor.

It appeared to Nic that for a moment Mr. Thomas lost some of the stoic composure he was trying desperately to maintain. His hand, for perhaps an inch or two, rose from his desk as if reaching out towards Willow, while his face softened slightly. Within a few seconds, though, the expression hardened once more and remained fixed. Nic was uncertain what to make of this behavior.

"My dear, my dear Willow, your loss has indeed been unfortunate. I expressed my deepest sympathies at the time of the accident and will do so again here. Your parents were upstanding members of the community, well respected. I realize this is painful for you, but a necessary step in the recovery process. Please continue."

Nic was uncertain what made him angrier, the mixed sense of sympathy the principal conveyed, or the pressure the man was placing on his friend to recount the horrible experience. He gritted his teeth and wondered how awful the "rehabilitation process" would become if he stood and punched the man in the face. He was soon surprised, however, at the strength Willow demonstrated by continuing.

"We went into the holo-room, but I asked Nic for the audio only. I don't really like the full immersion. Anyway, our project was on artificial intelligence." Mr. Thomas leaned forward further, his eyes narrowing as if attempting to bore into the girl.

"Everything seemed to be going fine, until we asked it about a test done a long time ago where a computer in the early days of artificial intelligence was asked if a man or a couple of horses were more valuable in a survival situation. The holo-face seemed to freak out. Well, more precisely, it sort of froze, and refused to answer any more questions."

Willow stopped to gather her thoughts, and the room went eerily silent. The principal was fully immersed in her story, unmoving. Even the barely perceptible twitching had disappeared. A whispery command escaped from his lips. "Go on."

"I'm not sure what else to say sir. Nic and I, we thought the situation just weird. So we wrapped up doing what we could and submitted the project findings the next day. Until now, I had almost forgotten the whole thing."

"I see."

The tension in the room eased as the principal let out a slow release of air and leaned back in thought. Mr. Thomas seemed relieved. Nic recalled that students like the Beast were brought to the principal's office for bad behavior. Some other kids also were hauled in, like the hackers who played with just about any console or outlet of interest to them. He found it strange that an event at the library, not even on school grounds, would be of such intense interest to the principal. Curious, he decided to ask.

"Mr. Thomas, I would like to know what we did wrong. We went to the library and asked a holo some questions about something that happened a long time ago. It's not like we tried to blow up the computer system there or anything."

The last comment from the boy elicited a sharp look from the principal which eventually subsided. "No, of course you didn't. Silly for you to even think such nonsense. Children, I think we have a case here of a simple misunderstanding. Somewhere, you have heard a tale of a man and some horses from a long time ago, probably something that is not even true. We do not know all that happened before the war and the rationing. A lot of the stories from that time are almost mythical. I am sorry children, this seems to be all a big misunderstanding. You are free to go back to class. I thank you for your time."

As they rose and left the room, Nic looked back into the principal's office. Mr. Thomas seemed drained, even defeated, as he wiped his forehead and sunk back into his chair. *It must be hard to run a school, even with today's technologies.* As they approached the admin bot who would escort them back to class, Willow spoke.

"Who would have thought that my parents' book would have led us on such an adventure, huh Nic? I never thought I would be so glad going back to class. Anything's better than that creepy office."

Nic Rocke   Marc Sherrod

Chapter Eight

Nic and Willow received a B+ for their Hist-science project presentation. The instructor bot gave them high marks for their accurate demonstration of how fossil fuels had nearly wiped out the planet until scientists had found a way to control fusion reaction and a few business pioneers had been able to make it commercially viable. Nic felt the bot was more than unfair, however, regarding docking them points for Willow's difficulty in presenting the material. Though she struggled, Nic was impressed by his friend's attempts to deliver their research. If the bot was capable to take into account her history as a human instructor would have, Nic was certain they would have scored higher. During her part, the rest of the classroom fell silent. There was much skepticism prior to her delivery that she would actually make it to the podium and say anything. When she finished, she gave a little smile and sat down. She performed well beyond anyone's expectations.

Nic found, after a few days of reflection, something was bothering him. He couldn't get the library holo's erratic behavior out of his mind. *Corrupted file? I don't believe it. There is more to this than something so simple. It's time to look into this.*

Reaching out to Bobby was his first consideration. The boy was a brilliant hacker. Asking for help, however, led nowhere. If the project was not a game, Bobby was simply not interested. From the mini-Screen his face seemed to wander further with each of Nic's pleas for help. It was clear he wanted to get back to his latest download and looked greatly relieved as Nic ended the call.

Willow crossed his mind as a possible collaborator for the investigation. After recalling the experience in the principal's office though, he decided against it. *Probably whatever I discover won't be anything important… but what if it is?* He felt a strong desire to protect her, to keep her away from any danger. *I'm on my own with this one.* With a deep sigh, he turned on the Screen and plunged in.

Though the buttons on the device were tiny, he preferred using them over enabling voice recognition, as most people did. Decades of research had gone into making progress on speech pattern detection, but the technology was not able to overcome differences in accents. Nuances in meaning and slang presented problems as well. It became a chore when using any device to speak directly and clearly to the computers as if they were small children. The speed at which the average person's fingers could input information was always faster than having to repeat something several times in order for even the more advanced machines to understand completely.

The most direct attempts yielded nothing. There were plenty of people out there with the first name of "Stephen" and the last name of "Butler" and all kinds of combinations, as well. It would take him a lifetime to go through all of the information.

Focusing on the time period was the next step, though he found the attempt no easier. Not knowing the exact date for the experiment regarding the question of the horses and the man, he had to use general dates. Nic decided that the first acknowledged examples of artificial intelligence research where computers beat humans in the ancient game of chess was too early. The arrival of the school Monitor and similar advanced systems of computer-based administration in different elements of society, he determined, was probably too late. That still left over half a century to explore. Nic let out a sigh. *It is going to be a long night.* He needed to narrow the search.

Going decade by decade from the middle of the century back took several hours. He used a variety of key words to search, including the obvious phrase "artificial intelligence." He also explored the names of several devices well-known for their heavy dependence on computer decision-making, including the craft sent to the outer planets and into interstellar space, and machines used in the home. *It's amazing that there was a time when people used to keep live animals as pets. Too messy, and too tragic once the pet died.*

After half the night spent searching, Nic shut down the device. There simply was no mention of the man, the experiment, nor any results from research regarding the subject of morality and computer decision-making. *It just doesn't make sense. Computers make all types of decisions now. Someone out there simply doesn't want the early years of artificial intelligence known.*

His mom's schedule finally flattened out, though not for the better. Late-night returns became the normal routine as her boss piled on even more work, now that she was fully trained in using all of the equipment at the factory. During his mom's absence, it only took a few days before Nic used all of his Screen credits in calling Willow; and even a call Nic placed to the local Ward Officer to obtain more credits resulted in nothing. The official was not convinced of his need for additional credits for supposed emergency medical reasons and promptly ended the call. Nic was ashamed for trying to come up with a fabrication to talk to Willow, but he was desperate and still very lonely. Nights became sleepless on these occasions when his mom called him to let him know the company was putting her up again in a hotel to be able stay later and start earlier. On a few occasions, Nic didn't even see his mom for several days, as their daily schedules became opposite to one another.

It was after a few weeks of this when Nic thought he was starting to lose his mind.

At first, the symptoms were infrequent and barely perceptible. Peripheral movement out of the corner of his eye revealed nothing extraordinary when he moved his head and looked about him to survey his surroundings on the walks home from school. Even the background chatter late at night as he went to sleep, he believed to be new uncaring neighbors in the complex, given the transitory nature to the place.

When the frequency of both the shadowy animations and upstairs noise increased, Nic became alarmed. He had heard sleep deprivation did strange things to the mind, and lately with his loneliness, he was not finding much time to rest. Worry became commonplace, almost obsessive. He didn't want his mom to worry about him, and he felt that the guys at school might be driven away if he were to open up. Most of all, he didn't want to lose his friendship with Willow, though several times he was a few seconds away from confiding in her. If he lost her because of his strange thoughts he knew the situation would become hopeless. Willow sensed something was wrong, but respected his silence.

Nic started feeling as if he were being followed, both when he left for school and from the moment he would head for home. The frequency at which he would come across Mr. Thomas in the hallway seemed on the rise, though by the time he would actually reach the point of crossing the principal's path he was certain an earlier, alarmed look had been replaced by stoic observance.

On one particularly restless night, Nic was startled to hear something large crash to the floor directly above his bed. After a few moments of scurrying, an absolute silence permeated his room. Nic believed he was within days of losing it altogether.

Such suspicions turned to certainty when he came across the same figure several times within a few days. He would come across the man, at least he thought of the figure as male, at different points in his daily routine. A heavy, thick coat and wide brimmed black hat hid the figure's true size and facial features. Nic was convinced he was even in the lunchroom at school, pretending to empty out some of the garbage receptacles. Yet even the worker's clothing and change to a small baseball-style cap pulled down low did little to reveal more about this mysterious person.

Running home in the rain one day, just after the mid-winter break, Nic stepped into a side street for a few minutes where one of the overhangs far above would provide some cover until the storm passed. He was shocked to find the stranger a mere few feet away watching him intently, but even more surprised when the stranger spoke in a whispery voice.

"Nic Rocke," the man began, "you have made a rather important discovery, something long forgotten. There are some out there who would have preferred what you have uncovered to have remained buried; for society to have let time pass to the point that no one would still be alive to remember. With what you have done, there is still hope. Take this." From under the folds of his coat the man produced a book. Old and weathered, it looked similar in age to the one in Willow's home they had used as the reference for their project. As the figure stepped away, he made a final comment. "Read through this book. All of it. The future of our society depends on it."

Before Nic could ask questions, the man disappeared.

During the walk back home, the encounter played over and over in Nic's mind. *Why am I involved? So much of this doesn't make any sense. How could a book be of such importance?* Confused, he doubled his pace, wanting to get off the street as soon as possible.

****

When Nic returned home, part of him wanted to throw the book away, but his moral compass deep within told him such a move would be foolish. He turned the volume over several times, examining the tattered edges. *It's older, much older, than the book at Willow's house. Smells strange too. I wonder, how long this book has been forgotten?*

Nic noticed the first few pages had fallen out. *Or had they been ripped out?* Nic looked for a title but was unable to find one. *Even the binding doesn't tell me anything. Title has been obscured.* Nic felt a prickly, icy sensation crawl up the back of his neck and grow into a blasting panic as he was able to make out the name of the author, barely legible at the dirtied bottom of the binding. *Stephen Butler.*

He felt dizzy, detached. It was like he was watching something on the Screen someone had made from the *Movie Star* download and had posted for everyone to see, except now it was he who was the star, and this was no simple movie.

Trying to read through the first several chapters proved difficult. All of the names were new to him. Some of the universities he had heard of, and several were still around; but the book was laden with terms he wasn't able to understand. After several attempts, he discovered at the end of the book, a section which listed all of the important terms in alphabetical order. His initial thrill at discovering he would be able to look up the author himself under "Butler, Stephen" was drowned when he saw the vast number of entries under this heading. Nic found the corresponding pages and attempted to read several; but, as before, there seemed to be an arcane vocabulary used to describe the events and he was able to gain very little.

For the first time in several weeks, Nic drifted off to sleep. The meeting with the strange man had made the unknown a tangible experience, and as disturbing as the meeting had been, Nic was assured he was not losing his mind. Reading through the book confirmed that he and Willow were on the verge of uncovering something big. Nic fell back into his bed. *I'll talk with her tomorrow about the book.* For now, a long sleep was needed to remove the fierce exhaustion which had plagued him.

Nic Rocke

Marc Sherrod

Chapter Nine

A giant holo hovered high up in the sky, overseeing the landscape. Its slow, monotonous rotation insured that it saw everything. The holo issued forth orders, but Nic couldn't hear what it was saying. Bots marched over the ground and soared through the sky, doing its bidding. Thousands of people tried to flee, but all were rounded up and pushed towards filthy cages. Nic thought he recognized among the horde several of the students from his school. He was certain he saw the face of his principal futilely trying to calm the crowd, but when he blinked, the face disappeared. All were wailing, trying to break free of the merciless machines. A terrifying sense of doom permeated the air.

Inside one of the cages, a man and a woman were desperately trying to break the lock. Despite being bruised and bloodied, they had not yet given up the fight. A sense of determination surrounded the two as they methodically picked at the mechanism. From out of the fleeing pack of humanity, a girl scuffled and broke free. She headed towards the cage and began helping the two adults inside. Though clearly scared, the girl repeatedly smashed the cage door with a rock, screaming as she did so. Her long, blond hair was swept to the side as her arm swung back for a crushing blow.

Two bots grabbed Nic from behind and pushed him violently towards a waiting cage. He struggled furiously but couldn't break their clenched steel grip. A wave of deep helplessness swam over him as he was thrown into the cell.

The alarm burned through his mind and brought him out of a catatonic existence. Nic panicked as he couldn't determine where he was, given his dulled senses. Recognition of his surroundings crept into his mind and familiarity replaced the strange dream as he rose to full consciousness. He tossed aside his sweat-soaked pillow as he made his way to the Screen to silence the noise. Despite not having any credits for outbound calls, he could still receive them. *Who is calling at this time? Some crank call probably. They're going to get it.*

As he prepared to scold the unwelcome intruder, Willow's face appeared. It was apparent she was terrified. Her eyes, swollen with tears, frantically searched for him to appear onscreen. Relief flooded her face as his image coalesced. For several seconds she made an attempt to speak, but was unable to do so. Nic knew he needed to calm her down. "Willow, just slow down. I can't understand anything," he began. "Take a few breaths, deep ones. Don't think of anything."

As her body reacted to the forced pacing of inhalation, Nic could see his friend quieting. After a few moments, she began again. This time, she was understandable. "It's awful; the whole place is upside down. Someone broke in, ruined everything. Oh Nic, even my parents' pictures are smashed."

Fear, anger and concern for his friend all welled within Nic simultaneously. It was hard for him to pick through his emotions and focus on Willow, who desperately needed his attention. All he could think of was her immediate safety. "Did they hurt you Willow? Are you okay?

"Yes Nic, I'm fine," the girl managed. "They must have done it while I was upstairs. I don't like the street noises so I use the headphones. But I couldn't sleep, so I went down there to read a book. I haven't been back in the closet since the day we did the project, but sometimes reading at night helps me sleep better. Especially the books my parents gave to me, it makes me feel close to them again. But the books were tossed everywhere. It's like someone was looking for something in a hurry."

Books. It struck him that the events of the day couldn't be simple coincidence. "Hang on Willow, I'll be right back." He went over to the side of his bed and picked up the old volume the strange man had given him. Leafing through it for a few seconds, he tucked it under his arm and returned to the front of the Screen. "I want you to do something for me," Nic said. "That book we used for our project, can you go find it?"

Willow looked around and steeled herself. She let out a deep sigh. "Uh-huh." After a few minutes, Willow returned. "I looked everywhere. All of the books were pulled off their shelves. But it's nowhere Nic. The other books are here. But that one's missing. I'm scared."

"Willow, listen to me. They came, found what they were looking for, and left. Someone wanted that book. I know it sounds crazy, but ever since we visited the library things have gotten weird. It's the middle of the night, but I've got to come over. This can't wait. I've got something to show you."

After several knocks Willow opened the door. It felt good to hold her in his arms, to try and comfort her as she softly sobbed, which caused his body to move gently with hers at each renewed cry. He noticed her hair smelled good as a scent of berries reached him. Unwillingly pulling away, Nic felt he had to survey the place.

Nic had expected Willow's apartment to have been roughed up, but his first glimpse of the apartment surprised him. Whoever had intruded had done a good job in going through everything and leaving a trail of destruction behind. He felt a wave of anger rush over him to see his friend distressed. It was clear after a few minutes that nothing was left to identify the thieves. He returned downstairs and pulled from his jacket the book the strange man had given to him the previous day. "I need you to do something for me," he asked. "You need to concentrate. Do you think you can find the notes we did for the Hist-science project?" Not understanding the reason for the request, but not questioning it either, Willow gave a slight nod of her head and went upstairs. She returned with her laptop and placed it on a table.

"Thanks," Nic said. "If I'm right this will only take a little while." Willow waited while Nic booted up the computer and sat down, scrolling through the various homework files. After a few moments he turned the laptop around and pointed to the screen. A knowing look stretched across his face. "Take a look."

Following her friend's request, Willow took the laptop in her hands and sat down in one of the living room chairs. "What is it I'm supposed to be noticing?"

"Your notes on the screen. See where you have marked the notes from your parents' book? '*The early days of artificial intelligence.*' That's what you have written."

"So?"

"Now scroll down. No, too far. Back up a bit. Yes, almost there. That's it. What do you see there?"

"It's my notes I was taking from the library. I tried to recall after we went there everything the holo-face mentioned. I couldn't remember much but I put down what I did recall."

Nic moved closer to his friend. Gently, he guided her hand to rest on two names apparent in the file.

"See here, then here. 'Steve B.' is the reference you have put down from your parents' book. He was the one who conducted the early experiments in artificial intelligence. Then this one over here. 'Steven Butler' is what you remembered from the holo-face."

Willow studied the two entries for a few moments, and then faced Nic with a startled expression. "This is not just a coincidence Nic. I don't think I like what I'm seeing here."

Nic nodded. "It gets stranger than that. Look at the name of the author on this book."

Willow's eyes widened. "What are we going to do?"

"I have an idea. We'll need to use your Screen." Nic input an address and waited. He expected he might wake his friends but the Screen instantly flashed on.

"Couldn't sleep?"

"Hi Conner. Got a problem. Hoped you could help."

From the expression on his face, Nic concluded that Conner assumed it involved Willow. He realized, given the disordered room and Willow's tear-stained face, that it must appear to Conner that they had a fight. A big one.

"I don't know Nic, not really good in that area." Conner was clearly uncomfortable, growing red and looking around.

"No, not that. We're okay. Well, not really." Nic decided it was best to change the subject, fast. "Look, I have something we don't understand. Remember our, uh, class project? We were following up and we were hoping you could help."

Relief flooded over Conner's face. Conner straightened and his confidence resumed. "Strange time to be doing homework, but whatever. You were right to contact us. Always can help a friend. Hey, guys, listen." Nic could see past Conner's image on the Screen Michael and Bobby designing one of Bobby's latest games. "So what's going on?"

Nic felt somewhat ashamed by the half-truth. Conner had, from the beginning, tried to help him get used to his new school. Nic tried to justify his call to his friend that technically this was an extension of his school project with Willow. Underneath however, he was concerned in bringing his friends into a situation that was becoming alarming. "Here it is." Nic held up the book to the Screen and flipped through a few pages.

"Hey, a book. Haven't seen one since the class field trip to the museum." For a few minutes Conner tried to read the pages but was unable to make out the fine print. "I can't tell from here what's written. Go ahead and replicate it."

Nic inserted the book open but face down in a slot underneath the screen. "These things probably don't do books anymore, but it will learn. Watch." Inside the replicator, tiny sensors moved around the book. Nic could see something was injected into the book itself. For a few minutes nothing else happened. The event was anti-climactic until Conner's shriek of triumph came through the Screen.

"Ha! I knew it could do it." said Conner, smiling, as he held up an exact copy of Butler's book and pushed it forward towards the Screen to show Nic. The Screen lens jiggled a little from the book's impact and Conner's image distorted momentarily but then self-corrected. "Even your old version, Nic. Hey guys, take a look."

Michael and Bobby seemed annoyed at the interruption but did as was instructed. For a few minutes no one said anything as they pored over the book. Then Bobby stopped at one page. He smiled when done reading. "Oh yes, Village Creek. That's where all the early A.I. work began," Bobby said in a matter-of-fact tone.

"You sure know your stuff," Michael said.

"I better. Grampy Gramps, I mean my grandfather," Bobby continued, looking a little embarrassed. "Well, that's what we used to call him. Anyway, he used to take me out there. Several times. Not much to see, but Butler's old place is probably still there. He's the one who got me interested in computers in the first place. Grampy was a great coder, worked out there."

"What?" Nic asked.

"Yeah, the best. 'Course that was back with petabytes, you know, the old stuff. Still, good ol' Grampy."

"No, the other thing you mentioned. You said you would go to Butler's place?"

"Oh. Him. That's Stephen Butler. Father of the early A.I. movement. Don't you know anything, Nic? The research facility is long gone but his house still stands. It's only about thirty minutes out of the city by mag-lev."

Nic didn't remember much of the conversation after that.

After the Screen call ended, Nic found Willow on the couch staring out the window. It seemed his friend's gaze was fixed on a distant object, unwavering. He needed to talk with her about what to do next, given Bobby's comments about Dr. Stephen Butler.

"I barely remember the countryside. We left when I was three. What Bobby said, it brought back some memories." Nic wasn't sure where she was going with this but sensed it was important for her to continue.

"I thought you lived in the city all your life?"

"No... I was born in Village Creek."

For a few moments neither of them spoke. "Willow, we have to go out there."

Chapter Ten

The mag-lev station appeared in the distance. Nic recalled the thrill he experienced when he rode the train for the first time around the age of five. His dad had taken him on the trip, and though the ride was short, he marveled at both the speed and the slight floating feeling he experienced as the train made its way across the countryside back east.

There was no one around. Being fully automated, the trains would run every twenty minutes. A rider would simply scan his or her mini-Screen across the scanner at the entrance and then board. Once inside the gates, they proceeded to their platform and took seats, waiting for their train. Nic noticed that they had about five minutes to wait. He didn't like being out in the open on the platform, as anyone would be able to see them.

Willow shivered next to him. Nic was unsure if it was because of the night chill or the toll the experience might be having on her. He draped his arm over his friend's shoulders, which she gratefully accepted. Nic looked down and noticed Willow's hand lay slightly curled, resting on her knee. He moved forward with his own to hold it, guided by his growing feelings for her.

"Nic," Willow whispered. As if broken from a trance, Nic looked into her face, hoping for a positive sign that might indicate any feelings she might have for him. He was surprised by her faraway gaze, concentrating on something further down the platform. "Is that the man you have been talking about? The one who gave you that old book?"

Slowly, Nic turned his head to the left and froze. The man was watching them, intently. Gradually, he raised a weapon and pointed it in their direction. Nic was already pulling Willow to the ground when he heard the man yell at them, ordering them down. *Why is he telling us to hit the ground if he plans to shoot us?* The alarm above indicated the train had entered into the station and would be arriving shortly.

A thunderous ripping noise erupted from behind them. Something exploded and sent debris in all directions. Shards of a destroyed chair pelted the two of them and Nic raised his jacket to protect them. Among the destruction, Nic thought he saw two shadowy figures move further down the platform as if in pursuit of the man. *The man is not trying to shoot us; he was aiming at those others.* The train came to a stop in front of them and the doors opened. He knew they wouldn't remain that way for long, and he grabbed Willow's arm.

"This is it. We have to go now!" The two of them bolted for the open door and fell into the train. Nic landed on his side. A searing pain shivered down his left arm from the impact. He struggled to get up as the train started pulling out of the station. Leaving the station was of no comfort. Willow was trembling from the experience, but otherwise unhurt. What concerned Nic most was the current location of the man, and his true intentions.

The train trip was uneventful. Willow had pulled herself within and was non-communicative. Nic tried several times to talk, but he realized she was mentally exhausted and it was better to leave her alone. He too, felt emotionally spent and physically drained. Several times he would crouch at both ends of the train car and peer into the next, but each time all that was revealed was an empty car. The experience was further tiring him, but he decided they had come too far to go back now. He had gained an appreciation that the situation had now become extremely dangerous, but he resolved that they must see this to the end.

As the train pulled into their destination, Willow stirred. She stood and looked in his direction. He could see her resolve and admired her strength. Nic looked in both directions before stepping onto the platform from the open door.

From the shadows emerged the strange man. *So, he is following us.* Unsure of what to do, Nic instinctively pushed Willow behind him, putting himself between the stranger and the girl. Given time, Willow might be able to make it to the other side of the platform and out of the station if he could hold the man here long enough.

"I wish you no harm, Nic Rocke. If I wanted to kill you I could have done so on several occasions."

The stranger removed a pack from around his shoulders and carefully set it on the ground. From the inside he pulled out a dirtied object and set it next to the pack. It looked as if five balls were tethered together by cords, or cables. "Cluster bomb. Highly effective." The man said this without any emotion. Nic realized he was a professional, but he thought it was better not to know exactly which field. "You really have no choice. You have to trust me. "They are called Guardians. Sent here to kill you. You have learned too much, Nic Rocke. At least in the minds of... some. I am here to protect you." The man shoved a device onto the bomb which loudly clicked into place.

Nic sized up the stranger. He realized it would have been easy for this professional to have taken him out by now. The chase from the Guardians proved that this was going to be far more difficult than Nic had expected. He decided the help was critical to their success. "All right. Which direction?"

"This way. If we take the south exit we'll find a hill. We keep going from there for five minutes. Only house around, can't miss it." Outside the mag-lev station, the man tapped Nic on the shoulder. He studied the land for a few minutes, looking doubtful. "It won't work if we stay together. There is no way we can make it across the open plain against them. They were sent for you, but for now, they will consider the bomb to be a greater threat. Go with her."

Nic watched as the man looked around a corner and sprinted. He reached a fence and waited. After several minutes, the two Guardians arrived. The man led them on a chase away from Nic and Willow. Nic realized the man was not coming back. It was a one-way mission. He admired him for his courage and sense of self-sacrifice.

Even with the thick barrier in between, the detonation forced them off their feet and slammed them to the dirt. For a few seconds, Nic was alarmed that Willow was possibly hurt. She stirred slightly and opened her eyes in his direction, but said nothing. Relieved, he stood and headed past the twisted metal of what was once the outer door to the mag-lev complex.

Ruined remains of the Guardians decorated the ground. Nic found the man a few feet away. The crumpled form confirmed he had been caught in the blast. "You are going to be challenged from now on in many ways," the man whispered. He pointed a trembling finger at Willow. "She's your strength. Keep her safe." The man's head rolled slightly to the side, and then stopped. Nic picked up the man's hat and placed it over his face. He wished there was time for a more formal ceremony but he knew he needed to act, fast. *Other Guardians might be in the area.*

"Let's go." Finding Willow, he gently slipped his hand into hers and headed for the hill. Just beyond, the house stood waiting.

Nic was amazed at the size of the house. The sprawling mansion overlooked the surrounding countryside, dwarfing the small trees which dotted the landscape. A thin river wound its way in the back and headed off to a clump of trees in the distance. The mansion was completely dark. After announcing themselves several times at the front door, there was still no response. Either the home system was completely shut down or, even worse, it was compromised.

After walking around the house several times, Nic turned to Willow. "We have to go in." His intention to break in was not lost on Willow.

"You want to do what? I don't think Dr. Butler will appreciate that Nic."

"I know, but what else are we going to do? Besides, there could be more of those Guardians around." Nic tried several windows on the first floor. All were shut. He could break one of them but decided there must be another way in. A small ladder on the south side of the house tilted up against the home. Nic grabbed it and found it was heavy. Willow grabbed the other end and they tried several windows. On their third try they found one of the windows was unlocked.

"Almost too convenient. I saw an old movie once where two men, I think they called them 'robbers,' did something like this. They tried to get into the house to steal something. Can you imagine if the security system were enabled right now what it could do? Tangle cables, knock out spray, maybe even –" whispered Nic.

"Saw that one too. Let's just get inside, okay Nic? I don't like it out here."

"You're right. Ready to climb? Stay just inside the window until I get there." Nic held the ladder while Willow ascended. Once he heard her drop safely on the other side, he climbed.

The two of them searched the room. It appeared to be a library full of old books, not very different from the room of books in Willow's home. Nic picked up a picture. Dr. Butler stood next to a computer, with several other men surrounding him. The edges of the picture were worn.

"I don't get it," Willow said. "There seems to be no one here."

"This house is huge. It is going to take us a long time to go through every room. I don't really like the idea, but we can't stay here for hours. What if we split up, maybe keep within shouting distance? What do you think?" A momentary fear crossed Willow's face but was replaced by a strong determination. "Just call if you need my help, okay?"

"Sure Nic. Or maybe you should call if you need mine." Willow managed a weak smile as she headed off.

After searching several rooms, Nic came up with nothing. The rooms were dusty; the house had an old smell. If Stephen Butler had lived here, it was a long time ago. He called out to Willow, but there was no response. He began to grow concerned. Nic searched the adjacent rooms but there was no sign of Willow. He cursed himself for having left her alone to scout ahead. Retracing his steps, he turned the corner and started to head back up the stairs. An evil snickering sound caught his attention before he reached halfway.

"Going back up so soon?" a voice called out from the blackness. "Just as I thought, Nic. You really are a coward after all." Nic froze on the stairway and slowly turned around. Along the far wall emerged the Beast holding the limp form of Willow in both hands. Rage burned deep within Nic as he saw his friend at the mercy of the hated behemoth. He headed back down the stairs, watching his enemy as he cautiously approached.

"That's right, come on back. We aren't through yet."

The Beast dropped Willow like an unwanted doll. Fortunately her head did not hit the ground but her body crumpled against the wall and remained motionless. The urge to rush to her side welled within Nic, but he suppressed it and faced the hulk.

"You just don't get it, do you Nic? See, I'm there for a reason. We're all over, in every school. Some things people aren't meant to understand. We have to stop those like you. Nosey, poking your head into things you shouldn't know. You aren't the first."

Nic looked around. "This is all a lie, then?"

"Yep, pretty good one too. You were careless, leaving a trace everywhere. It was easy for them to find you from all of your

Screen time searching for Dr. Butler. You know, I heard he's been dead a long time."

"Why do you do it?" Nic snapped. "Must have been a lot of money to pay you off. Or maybe it wasn't. All those medals. Did you win those medals or did you get a little help, Jacob?"

The Beast snarled in response. Nic could feel the hate pouring fourth. "Shut your mouth! And don't ever call me that!" *Good. He's getting mad, just a little more and he'll lose control. He's strong, but not really smart.* "Tell me why you're such a jerk in school. Oh, I know, you beat up on people smaller than you 'cause it makes you feel good. Big tough Jacob."

"You're gonna die for that!"

"Yeah? Come get me, but you don't have what it takes. Everyone knows it. Down deep, nothing is there." Nic deliberately turned his back and heard the yell of anger. The Beast charged.

Holding off moving until the last moment was difficult, but Nic waited until he was sure the Beast wouldn't be able to stop. Nic rolled away as the Beast's arms surged forward. It was then the Beast realized his mistake, for the basement wall was visible now that he was right in front of it. He crashed with a violent force into the wall. The Beast staggered, stumbled a few steps, and then keeled over. He didn't get back up.

Nic rushed over to Willow's side. She moaned softly, a welcome sign. He carried her through the front door struggling with fatigue. "Thank you Nic," she was able to manage. "Maybe we can go home now?"

Home. It seemed like a faraway place to Nic. Delicately lifting Willow, he then put his arm around the girl's waist. He met her look of surprise with a smile. "To help you back home; nothing else."

"Uh-huh." Willow smiled back.

****

When he returned home, it was already late morning. The entire trip had taken all night. Mom was there, waiting. There was no use trying to go straight to his room.

"Problems, honey?" she asked. He could tell she was genuinely concerned, and maybe even a little scared. She would yell when she was unhappy, but she was uncertain when really worried.

"Yeah, maybe a few Mom." His mother approached him. Nic waited for the assault of questions but only one came.

"Girl trouble? Maybe you and your little friend, Willow?" Nic didn't expect the conversation to go in that direction. He thought at first admitting to this would be a lie he could use to throw his mom off the real reason, but realized there was some truth to her question.

"I guess so," he admitted, realizing this had come out before he could stop it.

"You know you can talk to me about those things."

Nic paused and considered what she said. "I know Mom, but I think I will be all right." He turned to go to his room, but looked back at her. "Thanks for asking."

Nic Rocke

Marc Sherrod

Chapter Eleven

During the days after the visit to Butler's house, nothing happened. Though Nic found himself constantly looking over his shoulder, no shadows played tricks in his eyes. Even the holos at the library research center for class projects acted fine. It was as if things had become too normal.

Nic had thought it best to leave Willow alone during this time. Though he wanted terribly to contact her, he knew she had to take some time to deal with everything. He found himself struggling at times, trying to process all of the events.

It was during his next homeroom class when he realized not everything was back to its routine. The Beast had simply vanished. His innocent inquiries with some of his classmates resulted in blank stares. On one occasion, one of the girls responded with wide eyes, a brisk shaking of the head and a quick departure. Nic found her behavior odd. About a week after his return from Butler's home, Conner provided an answer during a conversation on the Screen. It was, however, something Nic found disturbing. "It's not something really discussed much. It just happens from time to time."

"What does?"

Conner looked thoughtful for a moment and responded. "A kid disappearing. Here, there. Oh, some people you hear about. Like you, and me, moving to a new location. That happens all the time. But there are other times, well, you just don't know."

"Doesn't that bother you?"

"Not really. It's happened as far back as I can remember. Just one of those things. You'll find though that some kids don't like to talk about it. Rumors, you know. I never trusted them, they seemed to be unbelievable." Conner could see that Nic was not taking it too well.

"Hey, cheer up. The Beast is gone. Isn't this a good thing? Or do you miss the constant threat of smelling like the toilet each time you walk in there, not knowing if he's scheduled you for a poo shampoo?" After Conner found he was the only one laughing, he tried again to reassure Nic. "Come on, Nic. Let it go. We have no control over it. Just be glad it hasn't happened to you. Didn't this happen back east at all?"

"That's what bothers me most. Looking back, it happened there, too. I just never noticed."

Chapter Twelve

*I can't stop thinking about the Beast. He's just…
disappeared. No one seems to care. Even Connor isn't worried.
Does no one ever question this sort of thing? Since no one at school
will talk about it, I'll need to find out on my own.*

Unfortunately, the Screen was not very helpful. He had little
to search with outside of a name and a description. Nic had been
able to log onto the school district's database and produce a few
class pictures from elementary school several years ago. A boy who
vaguely resembled Jake, even towering then, appeared on screen.
These mainly showed the Beast in competition, usually destroying
someone. There was no mention of names though, only pictures.
*So if that was him, he was good even back then. Was the Beast
chosen long ago and developed purposefully into the watchdog he
became?*

Several hours later, Nic felt he had wasted his time. Blogs,
chat sites, online gaming, nothing. There was absolutely no trace of

the Beast. He looked the next day as well, but with similar results. Frustrated, he stopped searching at home on the Screen. There were a few students at school who knew the Beast, and he asked them about him as a last ditch measure, earning only stern expressions from some of the admin bots who happened to be within hearing distance when he inquired.

On the last day before spring break, he confided in Willow at lunch. The bell had rung and his friends were already heading to their classes. "He's nowhere. Vanished. I've looked for hours and no one seems to want to talk about him."

"I know Nic. I just get weird looks too, when I ask. One of the bots even seemed like it was shaking its head at me. Something's not right."

Chapter Thirteen

During spring break, Nic's mother kept him busy with chores around the house. He asked her several times about upgrading their home computer systems, but always received the same reply. Nic hoped a better system might yield better results in his search for the Beast. "We just don't have that many credits coming in, Nic. Sorry, honey. Maybe next year. I can see if you could pick up a few hours at the plant." *Next year. Just as good as never happening. Besides, I know the kind of work you have to go through. Based on your exhausted state most of the time and occasional crying in the middle of the night, working at the plant is not something I want to do.*

****

School would resume the next day. Nic found himself leafing through the book on artificial intelligence the man had given him. He knew there must be clues in the book; he just didn't have the experience nor the knowledge to know what to pursue. The book reminded him of his latest adventure. It also brought back thoughts of her. *Willow.*

He had talked with her before the break and therefore he knew she was okay. He had no credits and assumed she must not have any either, as he received no Screen calls from her during the break. Or... the thought troubled him. *Perhaps she doesn't want to talk to me anymore. Our experiences had been traumatic. Maybe after all she has been through, she no longer wants to see me.* He could understand it, but didn't want to believe it. The thought of losing her burned deep within him. Nic wasn't able to wait until the next day at school to see her. He created an excuse for his mom so he could go out, and decided to walk the two miles to her home.

It was late in the afternoon when he arrived. After several attempts at the door, there was no response. He tried the link again, and this time spoke. "Willow, open the door. Please. I want to see you. I... need to see you."

As he headed away from the entrance to return home, a slight click behind him indicated that the door was open. Just inside he could see Willow's slight figure. Her head was downcast but he thought her eyes were looking in his direction.

Nic returned to the entrance and stood a few feet from her. Willow wouldn't move. He wasn't sure what to say, but he knew she was waiting for him. "I was worried. Maybe, you didn't want to see me anymore. I still can't believe everything that happened. With the Beast gone and all the rumors. I just –"

"Nic."

His rambling stopped at her soft whisper. All he could do was look at her, straight into her eyes which returned his gaze. "What?"

"Shh." She brought her finger up and lightly touched his lips. The door opened further and she took a step back. With a slight nod of her head to the right, she welcomed him.

"I'm not sure what we do now."

"Neither am I, Nic."

Nic Rocke

Chapter Fourteen

The evening spent at Willow's was calming. For most of the time they sat in silence, listening to the gentle rain splash across the windows. Willow had done a good job tidying up her place. He noticed the pictures of her parents had been repaired.

"They're connected, aren't they?" asked Willow.

"What are?"

"Going to Butler's house and the break in here. The visit to the Principal's office."

Nic didn't know how to respond. He had thought so too, but didn't want to scare his friend. *But now that she is thinking the same...* "Yes, I think so. Too many weird things have happened since the night we went out there." Willow stiffened. Nic thought she let out a little sob. Before he could go to her, she straightened and closed her eyes. "We just have to deal with it. Right, Nic?"

Nic couldn't say anything. He just nodded his head. *But what can we do?*

****

Nic was getting used to the Beast's absence at school. He started to look at the place through different eyes. Not having to worry about a predator potentially around the corner allowed him to focus on his school work. Once his grades started improving, his mom seemed to relax a little. Nic couldn't do anything about her work environment, but at least his mom didn't have to worry about him. He wondered if she secretly feared he would end up like her. Strange books and shadowy people were becoming a distant memory. Going to school was now enjoyable.

Then things became weird again.

Nic had never considered himself to be athletic. While he enjoyed playing catch with a cyber-ball with his dad when he was younger, he had never joined any organized sports. There simply hadn't been enough time with his mom's work schedule to devote himself to the long hours required for practice during the week, and the countless mag-lev rides on the weekends, to play against teams in distant locations.

He wasn't sure how to react when he found himself being recruited for the school's basebasket team. At first, a couple of the better-known players had started recognizing his presence in the hallways. Nic had assumed their greeting must have been intended for someone else until he looked behind him and saw no one.

Michael could give him no answer regarding the reason why this might be happening. He knew a couple of the athletes through some of the sports he played with them. Nic assumed the athletes were toying with him. After a week though, of no threats, he grew puzzled, but was no longer anxious. "The basebasket coach is looking for you," Michael mentioned at lunch one day. "He asked about you. Better start getting in shape."

Conner looked at Nic with a sense of awe, and even Bobby turned his head away from his mini-Screen for a few seconds to consider this turn of events. Nic noticed a few students at a nearby table must have overhead Michael, as they too, were looking at him. Willow said nothing, though he knew her gaze well enough to know she was also considering carefully this piece of surprising news.

"I don't even understand the rules of the game," Nic responded.

"It's actually pretty simple; you have nothing to worry about. I can show you. We could practice after school."

"But why me?"

No one at the table had an answer. The chime sounded, indicating lunch was over. "I don't know, Nic," Michael concluded. "He must see real potential in you." Within a week, two of the basebasket players asked Nic to take a few minutes and come with them. *This is it, I'm about to be tricked again.*

Instead of leading him to some hidden corner of the school to beat him up, the students took a turn in the halls and headed for the gyms. Nic had gone through this part of the school only once before, having gotten lost on his first day. "Wait here," one of the players ordered. It seemed to take a long time before they returned. Their blank expressions revealed nothing. "Follow us." They continued forward for a minute and came to an abrupt halt. Nic looked up and read the sign overhead. He realized he had arrived at the office of the coach of the basebasket team.

Nic remembered the last time he had been in a school administrator's suite. The visit with Willow to see the principal echoed bitterly. He hoped this time the meeting would go much better. With a sigh he gathered strength, and with the two players, he crossed the dreaded invisible barrier Nic imagined existed at every school administrator's door.

After entering, Nic looked around the room. Just about every kind of trophy decorated the office. Some were quite old, and a few could have used a cleaning. The place had an old smell to it. It wasn't a bad scent; if anything, it created a sense of wonder. Nic had experienced this once before, on a school trip to old D.C., the site of the nation's first capitol. There, the buildings seemed to speak to him, to tell them their history. This room gave him a similar feeling. The eyes of the players in the pictures from a long time ago looked out towards him, beckoning, even challenging him. He noticed great pride on those faces from long ago.

"Inspiring, isn't it?" The gruff voice from behind him caused Nic to whirl around. "Nice move son, it would be interesting to see you use that on the court." The man in front of Nic was a little taller than him. It was clear he continued to stay in shape. The coach reminded Nic of a solid brick on one of the old buildings in D.C. Old, but enduring. "Have a seat."

The coach looked at him, but said nothing. *Sizing me up,* Nic thought. *Why am I even here?*

After a few seconds of awkward silence, the man began again. "Rocke, Nic. First year here, transfer from the east coast.

No previous athletic experience, no involvement in anything here at the school outside of coming to classes. No tardies, no behavioral problems, except one visit to the principal's office three months ago." It was uncomfortable to hear the coach read off the details, demonstrating how much he already knew about him. That the man had all of this memorized was even worse. "We could go on. Nothing really remarkable is there? So why have I brought you here?"

Nic pondered, but couldn't think of any valid reason. The memory of the dreaded principal's office visit flooded back to him.

"Speak up son, I don't intend for this to be a one-way conversation."

Again, Nic considered. Down deep, he had nothing remarkable to offer. The strength and speed demonstrated by the players moving on the screens in this athletic office were far beyond anything he had to offer. "I really don't know, sir. To be honest, I was wondering the same thing."

"What was that? Don't mumble, it won't get you anywhere in life."

Nic knew the man was challenging him. He'd been clear enough for someone across the room to have heard. Nic didn't like the way this was going. "I said, I don't know. What you mentioned about me is true. Nothing remarkable."

"I see." The coach stood and went to one of the trophies. He brought it back and slammed it down on the old wooden desk in front of him. Nic could see some of the dust from the trophy fall onto the floor. "Pick it up."

"What?"

"You heard me. I'm not the one in this room who mumbles. Take it. Now."

Nic reached out and lifted the award. It was surprisingly heavy. He realized it must be made out of real metal, before nano-science made everything cheaper and stronger. He looked at the players. Like in the other pictures, all demonstrated a calm strength, an inner sense of confidence. One of the players looked like the coach, but a much younger version of him. He wondered if it was coincidence the man had picked up this particular trophy. He started to remove some of the dust to get a better look.

"Don't do that. It's better that way. I have a question for you. Why do you think they were State Champions?"

"I don't know. Maybe they were fast."

"No. Try again."

"Strength?"

"Are you stating the reason or asking me for it? You don't sound too sure."

Nic found he was growing irritated. He didn't see where this conversation was going. If the coach wanted him to play for the team, he should just come out and say it. "They practiced well." Nic knew he sounded more irritated than he would have liked.

The coach looked directly at Nic. A slight smile crossed his face. "Annoyance. Good. It's a start." The man snatched back the trophy and placed it on the shelf. "Your friend Michael speaks highly of you. When an athlete here has something to say, I listen. You see, he has proved himself. That one has character. My question for you, is, what kind of person are you?"

The inquiry seemed strange. Nic realized he had never been asked this type of question before. The conversation was full of questions he was not really sure how to answer.

"Time for you to head back to class. I want you to consider that last one. Some think you have potential. Maybe. Maybe not. You're going to have to prove it to me. It's an honor son, to represent this school as those before you have done. I believe you might have an interest in this sort of thing, it's just you have never been given the chance before. Think about what we have discussed here."

Nic rose and headed to the door. He wasn't sure if he should say goodbye or not. "Mumbling. They didn't mumble."

"What?" Nic asked.

"That's why those teams did well. I will see you again, Mr. Rocke."

Nic Rocke

Chapter Fifteen

Nic lay on his bed at home weighing his conversation with the coach. He could still see all of the trophies and smell the mustiness to the room. He wondered what it would feel like to have students years from now look at a picture of him on a trophy.

Pictures. He still had a few of them from back east. Nic slowly opened one of the drawers on his dresser and dug around the piles. Underneath some old clothing his search ended.

It must have been when he was five or six. Tucked under his left arm was the cyber-ball. His dad stood next to him, very tired but happy from the game of catch. Nic recalled the day was a pleasant one. It wasn't long after his dad disappeared. He hadn't looked at the picture for several years. For a while it brought back too many memories and at his young age everything was difficult to process.

His dad had never been an athlete, spending all of his time towards indoor pursuits. His work was something in the field of math or science. It was hard for Nic to remember the details. He asked his mother long ago about his dad's work. She didn't seem willing to discuss the past. Ever since, Nic didn't ask her about those earlier days.

Once, when out for ice cream, his dad asked him what he wanted to be when he grew up. He remembered responding that he wanted to do just what his dad was doing, even though he really didn't have a solid idea of what that was. His dad looked reflective, perhaps even a little sad at the time. "Is that what you really want?" his dad had asked, after explaining to Nic that he spent many hours trying to make machines work more efficiently.

"Well, you do it and enjoy it, right Dad?" Nic remembered asking him.

"Do it, yes," his dad responded. "Enjoy it? Perhaps once I did…"

Nic remembered as they finished their dessert, his advice to his son was to follow his dreams, whatever those may be. He realized his dad would have been proud of him in joining a high school team. Perhaps Willow would come to some of the games. Nic made his decision. He would see the coach tomorrow.

Chapter Sixteen

"That's great news, Nic. Congratulations." Conner was the first to shake his hand at the lunch table. Michael nodded in agreement, and Nic thought he heard Bobby mumble something positive about his invitation to join the team. Several of his classmates clapped him on the back. A few of the girls smiled. Nic hardly remembered their names, but they all now knew his.

The chime sounded. Each student got up and left. Only Nic and Willow remained. "That's great, Nic. Big change for you."

"Thanks." Willow grew silent. He could tell from her glancing around the room that she wanted to say something more. "Okay, something's up. They don't know you like I do. What do you want to say?"

"How can you tell?"

"Your eyes Willow. They keep going around. Like this. Watch." Nic swung his head in a wide, exaggerated loop, several times. He stopped when he heard her begin to giggle.

"They do not. You look silly."

"No, they really do that. Now, just tell me what you wanted to say."

Willow's smile quickly faded. A more serious expression with a hint of fear threw a shadow across her face. "Nic..."

He grew alarmed at her expression and sudden change in tone. "What is it? You know you can trust me."

"Yes. I can. I have a big change too. Maybe. The math test, just after the break, remember?"

"Sure. I think I actually passed it."

"Yes, well, I did too. In fact, it seems I did really well. The teacher actually interviewed me."

"That's great! They only do that when they are considering moving you up to the next level."

"Right. I always wanted this to happen. It means so much to me."

Nic could sense Willow's hesitation. After a few seconds he reached out and lifted her chin. He brought her eyes up to look into his. "This should be a good thing. Why are you so worried?"

"Because."

"You can tell me."

"We won't be together in homeroom anymore."

"Oh."

The two sat in silence in the empty cafeteria. Nic hadn't realized the repercussions taking the different class would have on her overall schedule. He felt his mood dropping at the news. Her presence was what he looked forward to when coming to school. It would be unfair of him to say anything to dissuade his friend from following her dreams.

"If I do this, we will still be able to see each other at lunch though, right Nic?"

"Of course."

"Good. 'Cause I don't think I would be able to stand it if we couldn't. I'll see you later." She leaned over and pressed a small kiss against his cheek. He could feel his face still tingling later that day at home.

Nic Rocke

Marc Sherrod

Chapter Seventeen

Michael spent the week before the start of the basebasket season working with Nic on teaching him the rules and practicing swinging the bat. They also went for jogs early in the morning before school. In the evening, Nic would fall asleep doing his homework, exhausted from all of the physical exercise.

Nic was surprised the sport had actually been two distinct sports a long time ago. When Michael compared the old rules of the two sports to the current basebasket rules, Nic couldn't understand how anyone could have enjoyed the sports of decades past. There was no greater sense of accomplishment than hitting the ball hard enough with the bat and watching it sail past the vain attempts of the other team members to stop it before it plunged into the homerun hole. He was convinced a rubbery ball, which bounced on the court wouldn't give him the satisfaction the metallic cyber-ball did as it flew from the bat, shrieking across the court.

The day prior to the first day of the season, when all of the team's athletes would gather for the first practice, Michael pulled him aside. "I've done all I can Nic, but I must admit, I'm puzzled. The coach must really see some potential in you."

"Is that a compliment?" Nic asked.

"Well, no. You can take it to be one though."

Nic stopped running and looked at his friend. "Not telling me how you feel isn't going to make me any better. I need to know the truth."

"Is that what you really want?"

"Yes. I think so." Nic started to regret his decision. *Am I really that bad at this game?*

"You're right, you deserve that at least," Michael said. "The truth is, you suck."

The comment stung. Nic started to protest, but he realized his friend was telling him something he already knew. When he had found footage on the Screen of high school athletes performing the sport, he knew they were way beyond his skill level. Some of them had been playing this game since they were half his age. "What's the use," Nic whispered. "I'm just going to be laughed at tomorrow."

"Maybe," Michael commented. "Don't let it get to you, though. That happened to me when I first started hover-soccer. I just pushed through it. Whatever they said, it didn't matter. When I got good, they shut up."

"But when was that... third grade?" Nic asked.

"Yeah, about then. It's true, I was a lot younger." Nic looked at the ground and angrily kicked a few stones. Michael didn't know how to cheer up his friend. He decided to try a different way. "Look, in the end it won't matter what anyone thinks. It's really just about what you feel. You don't have to worry. She won't be worrying."

An awkward few seconds followed. Nic was in disbelief of his friend's comments. "What did you just say?"

"I've been there before. You think they care, but they really don't. You could almost poop in your pants out there just being nervous the first time on the field, but all they see is you, in your uniform, looking like a man. After your first game, you don't feel nervous anymore. Even if you get crushed out there, girls don't care about the score. So don't worry."

"She?"

"Yeah, she. Willow. What's the big deal? I figured since you guys hang out a lot, she must be... you know... your girlfriend."

Nic turned the color of the sweat-stained crimson shirt he was wearing. He wondered how many at school thought this. If he didn't do something soon, his actions would confirm it for Michael. It bothered him others would assume certain things about them when he was still unsure of his own feelings.

"No, not my girlfriend. We just study together sometimes, like that one project for class." Nic decided the less he said about that event, the better, as it had led to an adventure that had almost got the two of them killed. He felt in some way he was pushing Willow away with this denial, but he believed this was the best thing to say, for now. Nic didn't want any rumors getting back to Willow that he told Michael she was his girlfriend. What if she didn't feel the same? "Anyway, let's keep going. I don't always want to suck at this sport."

"Sorry I was blunt. Hey, I know that coach. It's not his style to put you in a situation you can't handle. You saw his trophies; he's had some great teams. He'll help make you better. You'll see."

****

Nic arrived at the first practice with great hesitation. Though Michael's words were encouraging, he still felt concern that he would look foolish out on the court. His fears were realized as he approached the field watching the players perform. He knew they were years ahead of him.

Before even seeing the players, he heard the sharp clanging of the bat. Watching videos with Michael as part of his training had taught him such a sound usually meant a good hit. When he swung, the sound his bat made was muted. It indicated a far weaker hit, resulting in a throw to first base for the out. It was difficult enough for him to visualize reaching first base, let alone trying to get all the way around to fifth base for the score. Michael had taught him the first step was just to hit safely with consistency, which he had yet to master.

He entered the court from the outfield. Players were making great leaps, pulling down incredible shots towards the home run hole with relative ease. Nic realized if he could jump half as high as they were, he would set his own personal best record.

The coach was waiting for him. Nic pretended not to notice, but he eyed the coach staring in his direction the moment he entered the court. The spongy clay of the court seemed to echo his footsteps. The shoes Michael had lent him were appropriate, though a little old. Nic felt all eyes must be on his noisy arrival, but when he looked around, the players were all concentrating on their own efforts.

"Good to see you made it Mr. Rocke," the coach said with his gruffy voice. "Let me check your footwear. If the shoes are no good, the player is no good. Doesn't matter how much training you do if you turn your ankle because of lousy shoes." The coach tapped his shoes several times. "Solid. Good. I remember this style, everyone had them. They'll work. Maybe a few years old."

Nic thought he heard snickering behind him, but when he turned to look, a small group of players had already moved away to go practice fielding.

"How are you feeling today?" the coach asked Nic.

Nic turned back at the unexpected question. "Fine."

"Did you eat before coming here?"

"Yes."

"Have you been practicing over the last week?"

"Yes."

"Do you always answer in monosyllables?" asked the coach.

"What?"

"Ha! Always gets 'em, never fails. It's a joke son, you can laugh. No need to be so nervous." Nic didn't feel like laughing. "Okay, head over to that group back there. I want to see you take a few swings."

Nic did as instructed. Michael mentioned the coach would try him out in a few different areas in order to make a thorough determination of his basic skills. He was hopeful he would be able to do well in at least one area today. Half an hour later, his hope had disappeared.

Hitting did not go well. At first, Nic was convinced the pitcher was tossing the ball at him unnecessarily fast until he looked at the next court over and saw other batters effortlessly sending balls much faster beyond the infield. Even when the coach put in another pitcher, someone obviously with far less skill than the first, Nic still couldn't connect with the ball. He was angry at himself and angry at Michael for making it look so easy. *Strike one.*

After his miserable performance trying to hit the ball, the coach put him in the infield. The ball came at him quickly. There wasn't much time to react, especially if the ball came at him directly. Grounders weren't any easier; he had to predict where the ball would eventually wind up after skipping along the ground.

The coach took the bat and asked one of the senior players to lob balls at him. The soft thudding sound let Nic know the balls weren't hit with much force, but they still seemed to come at him with terrific speed. The first, a grounder, rolled right up to him and at the last moment seemed to hop like a rabbit right above his outstretched glove into the outfield. Nic was certain he had guessed where the ball would be, but it seemed to take on a life of its own with the sole purpose of embarrassing him.

The next was a direct shot aimed right at Nic. He didn't need to worry about strange angles a rolling ball would take, but he was concerned about the speed. His glove reached up to grab the ball, which was sailing just a foot above his head. He felt the impact of the metal cyber-ball which crushed two of his fingers, sending him backwards and forcing him to drop it. A few of the players in the outfield looked up from their own practice and merely shook their heads. *Strike two.*

Nic's injured fingers throbbed horribly as he was sent next to the outfield. Of all the areas, Nic felt this was where he excelled. While he couldn't jump as high as the other players, he was certain his timing was good enough to be able to rob a batter of a good hit. If the ball was just above his head on its way to the home run hole, Nic felt confident he would be able to snatch it. Nic didn't realize that balls to the outfield could take many paths to get there.

The coach, once again at the batter's plate, sent the ball out towards Nic. Instead of the expected line drive shot, the ball was sent skyward in a high arc. Nic followed its path... until the ball simply disappeared. He panicked as he realized the ball was lost in the sunlight.

Nic Rocke Marc Sherrod

Chapter Eighteen

"What did you do then?" Willow asked.

"Nothing. I couldn't see it. I thought about everyone watching, especially the coach. If I moved, the ball might land wherever I was. So I just stood there."

Recounting the day's horrible practice to Willow was painful. The news had spread at school about Nic's performance. He called Willow so she could hear his side of the story; he was afraid that whatever she may have been told at school was greatly exaggerated. Nic realized, though, as the Screen call was going through, that the true story itself was bad enough and that any exaggeration probably couldn't make the situation worse. Still, he needed to talk to someone.

"Then it hit you."

With a sigh and a downward glance, Nic admitted the truth. "Yes. Right on the head. I went out cold. The next thing I knew, the coach was pouring water on me to wake me up."

"Oh Nic. I'm so sorry. How do you feel now?"

Nic hadn't seen Willow look so concerned before. Her genuine look of sympathy through her searching eyes touched him. He decided he had been right in making the call to her. "It's still sore. Feels like a tight knot up there. Coach says it will go away in a few days. Still wants me on the team. Don't know why."

"It was your first day. Give it time Nic, you'll improve. I think by the time the season starts, you'll be doing much better. Can't wait to see what your uniform looks like."

Nic recalled Michael's comments at practice about being out on the court in a uniform in front of girls. He changed the subject before Willow noticed he was becoming embarrassed. "So enough about me. How is the math class going?"

It's fine."

"Just fine? You've spent so much time on it."

A wide smile appeared on Willow's face. "Well," she said, "If you must know, I got an A on the test yesterday!"

Nic was happy to see Willow so excited about something. "Again? That's great. Must be four in a row now."

"Five," Willow corrected in a playful tone. "But who's counting? I also joined the judo club," she added. "So you better watch out or I'll throw you!"

"Wish I could be doing those things, but you're way out of my league now." A serious look fell across Willow's face. Her smile vanished and she looked thoughtful. Nic wondered why his comment seemed to trouble her.

"No, I'm not. I don't know if I would be in this class now if it hadn't been for you."

For several seconds neither of them said anything. The slight humming of the Screen was the only sound in the room.

"I miss not seeing you in the mornings." The words slipped out of Nic before he realized what he had said. The effect was immediate on Willow. Her body relaxed, the tenseness disappearing. She seemed in some way reassured.

"Well, it's getting late. Still have some of that math to do." Willow paused, her smile returning. "I'm glad we talked tonight Nic. Good night."

"See you tomorrow."

Nic Rocke

Marc Sherrod

Chapter Nineteen

At school the next day, it seemed to Nic as if he had swallowed a brick. The dull pain reminded him of one time when he had eaten something old. For several hours afterwards, his body had let him know it didn't agree with the contents. Earlier today, the home doctor diagnosis was a "case of the nerves." As before, the virtual doctor had informed him to consult other sources for more information. He gave the image of the medical professional a dirty look which seemed to have no impact on the halo. Still, he wondered if Bobby was right; did the program think he was stupid?

"A case of the nerves," Michael had commented. "I still get them. All the time."

"Is it bad?" Nic asked.

"No. It's normal. It's just your body's way of preparing to fight." Michael emphasized the last sentence with a couple of jabs as if he were fighting.

"When will it go away?"

"You're worrying now because you aren't at the game. I looked it up once; something called 'anticipatory anxiety.' Just means you are worrying about some event coming. For most people, you'll forget about it five minutes after the game begins. However, some people..."

"What?" Nic was concerned. Michael had a mischievous look on his face.

"One guy I knew, probably the worst case ever. Looked green before the game. Thought he would be better once we started playing, but he wasn't. Coach called him into the game to play midfield. He got up, swayed a little, and then puked all over himself. Once he woke up, coach still made him go play, with the puke still all over his uniform. Said it would make a man of him."

"Did it?"

"Not at first. He got a good nickname. Vomit Victor. He hated it."

"Great."

"He went on to become a star scorer, really determined. So maybe it was worth it."

****

In the dugout, the pain was not lessening. If anything, Nic felt it had increased. It was more acute, a stronger sense of stinging rather than a dull background annoyance. The coach approached. "Ready for the big game tonight, Nic?"

"Maybe."

"Son, there is no 'maybe' in this game. Either you are, or you aren't. Don't waste your time in life with half-heartedness."

Nic thought about this and tried to suppress the knot in his stomach. "Yes. I'm ready."

"Good. During warm up today, I want you to go to the pitcher's mound. Remember last Thursday? You started throwing the cyber-ball. Try that again today."

"Okay. But Smith might kick me off the mound again, like he did last week."

"No, he won't."

"How can you be sure? He told me no newbie screw-ups allowed. Smith looked pretty mad."

"He won't be." The coach gave Nic a sharp, reassuring look. "Trust me."

Nic walked over to the practice mounds as instructed. Several of the pitchers had arrived early and were already loosening up for the game. He admired their dedication.

"Hey Nic," one of the seniors called out. The greeting was completely unexpected. None of the seniors had ever acknowledged his presence, either on the court or in the school. One of the mounds was unoccupied. Someone even placed a bucket of cyber-balls next to it. Last week, Nic needed to go and get his own and heft them all the way back to the mound. It was an unwritten rule on the team for the early arrivers to display courtesy to their teammates by supplying their mounds with the buckets.

On the mound, Nic looked around him. He spotted Smith sitting off to the side. Nic realized this was the first time he ever saw Smith immobile. A glum expression was planted on his face, and his shoulders drooped. Nic recalled the coach's earlier words and wondered if the boy had been scolded.

Several of his practice pitches went wide. The robo catcher was able to adjust and sent the cyber-balls back to him. The feedback board behind the catcher displayed the speeds of his thrown cyber-balls. Some of the other information, such as wind direction, Nic ignored.

For several minutes he read the advice the feedback board was generating. A camera placed near the dugout had captured his performance and fed it into a software program for analysis. The notes in green were suggestions he should do to enhance his performance, whereas anything written in red was advice on what to stop doing. Nic was somewhat confused by the display. There were many more red comments than green. He was confused about what he should begin addressing first. "Don't spend too much time dwelling on it. Sometimes you get more confused the longer you think." Nic turned to face the direction where the comment had come. The coach had come from behind.

"The school paid a great amount of money for this thing. Everyone loved it. Good eye candy. I suppose to be fair it helps, some. No replacement though, for intuition."

Nic looked back at the display board and then again at the coach. He was still confused. "I don't know what to do."

"Good. That's exactly where you should be." The coach went over and picked up one of the cyber-balls. He casually lobbed it towards the robot catcher. On the display, the statistics for the throw lit it up in red and green. A much younger image of the coach appeared next to the statistics, as did a streaming list of accolades. Nic lost count how many times a championship was mentioned.

"I do need to have them update that picture. Don't look anything like that now. No matter, I can do that later. Anyway son, what do you see?"

Nic was lost. "A lot of games won, not so many losses."

"No, for the throw. Concentrate on the throw."

Nic studied the board. The comments in red and green were overwhelming. "There's a lot up there. Too much to take in. A pitcher could be here all day trying to do everything up there in red as performance suggestions."

"That's right, now you're getting it. Here, take the ball; I mean cyber-ball. Still have never got used to calling it that. Now throw it."

Nic did as his coach instructed. The throw wasn't particularly fast nor was it on target. Immediately, the feedback appeared, mostly in red. The list of suggestions scrolled several times before stopping. "What are you going to address first?"

"I don't know, there's so much up there."

"Let's try this a different way. Ignore what you see up there. You just threw the ball; your body still remembers the throw. What do you think you should do?"

Nic thought about how his shoulder ached. The pain was an indication of what he was doing wrong. "Maybe if I come a little more over the top, with my arm more extended."

"Good. I would agree. Try it."

Nic picked up another and threw it at home plate. Again, the feedback on the board scrolled, but with far different results. Comments in green and red were much more balanced. "Nice throw, son. Good form; and I bet your shoulder doesn't hurt anymore either.

The coach was right. Nic couldn't sense the dull ache. "How did you know that?"

"Well, I could tell you the board displayed it up there as item number twenty-five, but I only saw that after watching your form. Most pitchers would feel pain by throwing it the way you did. I did it that way too, sometimes. Pain has a funny way of making you stop doing something wrong."

Nic threw several more pitches with increasingly better results. "You learn fast, son. Sure you didn't play ball as a little feller a long time ago?"

"No, never had time. Mom was always busy at work. Played catch with my dad a lot though. He tried to teach me a few things about throwing."

"Hmm. I wonder."

"What?"

The coach walked over to a nearby bucket of cyber-balls and placed them at Nic's feet. "Think back to that time period. Do you remember anything?"

"Sure. Blue skies, warm days. My dad and I would get up early, sometimes be out there all morning. Mom would call out to us for lunch and we would be back in the yard as soon as we finished. Used to go to sleep wiped out, then we would do it all again. I can almost smell the grass now."

"Good memories. As it should be. Do you remember what he told you about throwing?"

Nic thought back, but had trouble remembering specific instructions. He could see his dad demonstrating the throws. Like Nic's recent pitch, his dad brought his arm up extended and high. "I can see him now, throwing like I just did. He threw well, we didn't have a robot practice catcher but the ball always went over the plate. He used to drop his glove just slightly, and then went into the wind up. High, over his head, body twisting around, and here comes the release. Wait, there it is, that's it!" Nic's shout rang across the practice courts. Several of the pitchers looked in his direction.

"What do you see?" asked the coach.

He opened his eyes and looked towards home plate. "My throw. I let go too early."

"Pick one up; try to throw like your dad did."

Nic took a cyber-ball and remembered again his dad's throw. He closed his eyes and went into the wind up. At the last moment he opened his eyes and imagined letting go of the cyber-ball at the same time his dad did. It made a satisfying thudding noise as the robot catcher captured it. Nic instinctively looked up towards the display board.

"No, close your eyes. How did it feel?"

Nic reviewed his throw. The form seemed good and the release seemed right on time. His shoulder felt fine. "Good. It felt good."

"If you need some unnecessary confirmation, take a look. Somebody else seems to agree." Nic looked up towards the display board. He had never seen so much feedback in green. The red comments were much fewer in comparison. One of the other pitchers yelled congratulations his way. "It was a good throw. Now empty that bucket. Try to throw the same way you just did. Remember the game's in twenty minutes."

"I wouldn't miss it, coach."

Chapter Twenty

The game was going well for the team. The first three innings were close, but then things changed quickly. Smith no longer looked depressed as he did prior to the game. He struck out three in the fifth inning and a few home run blasts put the team up 11-2. Nic found he was enjoying watching from the bullpen. He had never been this close to a game before.

The 7th inning was usually reserved for non-starter pitchers unless the game was close or one of the pitchers was pitching a no-hitter and still looked fine out there. Given the lopsided score, the coach put in one of the younger pitchers who continued the domination. The coach asked Nic to take his place on one of the practice mounds. Nic didn't think much about the move and started lobbing a few balls. This felt even better than just watching. Perhaps some of his classmates now saw him in uniform.

Two batters have already been struck out. It is going to be an early night at this pace. I wonder what I'll do when I get home...

At first, Nic didn't hear his name called. The coach had to make his way all the way to the bullpen himself. "Must have wax in your ears, son."

"Sorry?"

"Toss a couple more. Then head out there. You're up."

Nic couldn't believe what he had just heard. Instantly, his mood went from euphoric to anxious. The walk out to the mound seemed to take a long time. On the way, he thought he tasted his dinner again. Images of the player throwing up from Michael's story danced in his head.

The first few practice throws from the mound were wide. Several times the catcher had to jump out of the catcher's crouch to get to the ball. Nic imagined several people laughing in the crowd but when he looked up, all eyes seemed serious. This simply made the matter worse.

His first batter had not been doing well today. He had no hits and in fact, had struck out three of the four times he went to the plate already. After taking his stance, he swung the bat a few times. The catcher called for a low ball, not one Nic particularly liked. His throw was inside and high. A questioning look from the catcher was the result.

Again, a low ball was called. Nic managed to bring the throw closer to the center of the plate, but the throw was still too high. The batter connected and sent the cyber-ball sailing deep into the outfield. With little speed on the throw, it was an easy hit. The batter reached second base easily.

I want to be anywhere but here! Maybe if I fake an injury... no, that's not me. Come on, get it together!

The next batter approached the plate. This one was somewhat taller than the one before him. Unfortunately, he already had two hits for the day. Nic groaned inwardly. The call from the catcher was for high and inside. Nic felt this was much more doable given his previous pitches had been thrown high. As he released the cyber-ball, he realized he had let go too late. The ball was thrown too high to the inside, hitting the batter. The struck player trotted to first. *I look stupid out here.* A restless mood emerged among the crowd. The weight of all eyes on him added pressure. Anyone could be out there watching. Then it struck him. *Even Willow could be in the stands. She said she wanted to see me in my uniform.*

Nic could see from the grip on the cyber-ball that two of his fingers were bleeding. There were two players on base and he had yet to throw a strike. He was starting to lose both concentration and confidence. The next batter had been doing well. Nic started calculating how many runs he would have to give up before the coach ended this misery.

"Time!"

The exclamation from the home plate umpire startled Nic. Someone on one of the teams had called for a timeout. Nic saw his coach coming towards him slowly, methodically, from the dugout. He realized the wait to be pulled from the mound wasn't long. He picked up the cyber-ball and prepared to hand it to the coach.

"How ya doing out here?"

"Not good. Here you go." Nic began to hand over the ball. The coach politely refused it and with a brush of his hand gently pushed it back.

"Not here to take you out. I'm here to see how you think you can get out of this mess."

The unexpected statement caught Nic. "It's hard, more difficult than I thought it would be. Real batters, everyone watching. I keep thinking I'll blow it, and I am."

"Well see, that's the problem. You aren't thinking how to beat 'em. You're too wrapped up in thinking how not to put on a bad show. That's a different approach, one that never works."

Nic looked up into the stands. The crowd was subdued, wondering what effect the coach's talk would have on Nic. While a few in the crowd were wearing the colors of the opposing team, most were dressed in his high school's jerseys. "I guess I'm worried about them. Out there. But I guess they aren't the enemy. The only one I have to worry about is at the plate."

"Yep, you got it."

"It seems pretty far away from here to him though. Almost like I can't throw it that far with any accuracy."

"You want me to go measure it? He's no farther away than where you were throwing just a few hours ago." The coach started to count his paces. Nic realized he would walk all the way to the plate. The crowd began to stir, wondering what was happening. Nic thought the coach looked funny and began to laugh. At the sound the coach turned around. "Why don't you join me? Then you'll see I'm right."

"No, please stop. I get it."

The coach returned to Nic. "So, we come all the way around. You're still in a tight spot."

Renewed with confidence at his coach's support, Nick nodded. "Yeah, but I'll get him."

"Good. Just one other thing. Don't forget what you learned in practice. About your dad. Remember how you were throwing." The coach headed back to the dugout. The crowd was still watching but seemed to have relaxed.

"I can do this," Nic reminded himself.

After several balls and strikes, the count was full. Another ball and the batter would walk. Nic was determined not to let this happen. He remembered his dad's pitching form and sent the cyber-ball screaming to the plate. The batter swung high and missed it. *Strike three.* For several seconds Nic sat at the mound not fully believing what had happened. Several people in the stands got up to stretch. The mood was no longer anxious.

"Let's go, you can't stand out here all day." One of the outfielders had come up to Nic and clapped him on the back. Nic headed back to the dugout. The coach was going through a rotation and was putting one of the other younger pitchers on the mound for the next inning.

"Well done, Mr. Rocke," the coach mentioned as he looked up from his roster. "You have proved you have it in you."

Nic Rocke Marc Sherrod

Chapter Twenty-One

Winning the game was an incredible feeling. Though he had only pitched one out, the coach had trusted him. Nic had delivered. He noticed the other players were more approachable after the game. Even Smith seemed like a different person. Several smiled and congratulated him on finishing the inning.

Nic waited until after the game was long over to see if Willow had been in the stands. He scanned it several times as the fans were leaving the game, but didn't see her. Even when the cleanup bots were removing the garbage he remained on the field, looking for her. He realized it was wasted time but he had deeply wished that she had seen him play.

His walk back home was uneventful. *I'll call Willow from the Screen with my leftover credits. Mom will be thrilled to hear about the game, too. She needed to pick up an additional shift today, but should be home by now. Maybe tomorrow even some of the students I don't know well will look in my direction. Maybe I won't be dismissed anymore as just one of the nameless new students.*

It was odd when his mom was not waiting for him when he returned home. She gushed over his uniform when he brought it back for the first time and insisted he try it on for pictures. He felt his jaw would drop off with all of the smiling by the time she finished instructing the Screen to take the various shots.

A sweep through the apartment revealed nothing. There was no sign of her, nor any evidence she had returned home. He thought she might have grown tired waiting for his return, but she was neither in her bedroom nor on the couch. The usual signs showing her return were lacking. He checked in her closet for the uniform with the green tea stain on the right side, but it wasn't there. She'd worn this one in the morning when she headed off to the plant.

He walked past the Screen and thought about the call to Willow, which would need to wait. Something caught his eye. A blinking light indicated several received calls. The occasional call was not uncommon but several calls was highly unusual. They simply didn't know that many people. The ominous red flashing of the light and his mom's disappearance filled Nic with an uneasy feeling. The two events couldn't be a matter of coincidence.

Nic cycled through the calls.

"This call is for Nic Rocke," an automated voice began. "Please call the Saint Augustus hospital as soon as possible. This is an emergency."

The next one was more ominous.

"Mr. Rocke, this is Dr. Clemmons from Saint Augustus. Your mother has been in an industrial accident. It is imperative you contact us immediately."

Nic realized her injury must have occurred while he was walking back home from the game. He placed a return call through the Screen to the hospital and informed one of the holos he received the calls.

"Rocke, Nic" the holo confirmed his identity. The unmoving eyes seemed soulless, hollow. *How cruel. When I need help the most, this is what appears onscreen.*

"I received a call, my mom's been hurt. How can I-"

"No information can be given over the Screen. You must come to the hospital, immediately." The face remained insensitive, unmoving.

He was informed further that his age prevented him from receiving additional details. The holo inquired about the presence of any adults but Nic informed it there were none. The holo quickly, but thoroughly, reviewed basic details of his mom's insurance plan. Nic was informed he would need to find his own way to the hospital as services did not extend to "vehicular transportation." Most of the other details were lost on Nic.

Nic ended the call by punching the Screen. He almost destroyed it.

Shuttle service was the only option. Nic had ridden in a shuttle once before when he was much younger. He found the service through the Screen and determined it would require all of his remaining credits. The call to Willow would need to wait.

The hospital was a labyrinth of floors, elevators and doors. Even with all of the signage, it was easy to become lost. Nic asked several staff members for directions. Politely, but quickly, he would receive the answers. Once he arrived where directed, he would become lost again. Exhausted, he finally arrived at the floor where his mother was located. One sign read "radiation treatment." *How many people have been injured in this way?* With great apprehension, he proceeded through the main doors to the waiting area.

The room was full. A number of people were standing, as there were not enough seats. Several babies were crying, refusing to be consoled by their mothers. Everyone looked either miserable or anxious. One woman at the counter argued vainly with a holo. Nic was not able to understand the full details of the conversation, but apparently her insurance did not cover all of the treatments her husband needed.

The counter holo seemed to be waiting for him. Its lifeless eyes narrowed at his approach. There was no greeting, only a businesslike manner. "Name."

"Nic Rocke."

"Wait a moment." After a few minutes, a staff member unexpectedly came through one of the side doors headed for him. He realized the issue must be serious. Holos and bots handled routine transactions, but facilitating the more serious issues was reserved for human staff members.

"Dr. Clemmons." The comment was more matter-of-fact than greeting. If the man was not made of flesh, Nic would have thought he was speaking to a holo.

"Nic Rocke," he responded to the doctor. "What happened to my mom?"

Dr. Clemmons mentioned he was one of the hospital staff who specialized in industrial injuries. As with the experience of the home diagnosis holo treating his black eye from the Beast several months ago, Nic didn't understand the terminology the doctor used. He concluded this must be an unfortunate common practice both holos and humans used when talking with the public, but thought better not to interrupt the doctor, even though he felt it would be much more helpful if the doctor got to the point. The professional eventually did make a statement Nic could understand. "To summarize, she has suffered serious radiation burns. Recovery will require several weeks; she'll need to stay here. She will be evaluated routinely."

Nic considered the doctor's words carefully. Questions came into his consciousness one after another. "How could this have happened?"

The doctor appeared to choose his words before responding. "Industrial accidents of this kind are not uncommon."

Nic sensed he was not hearing the entire story. "Not uncommon? My mom used to talk about these accidents happening years ago. She mentioned recently though, that with current safety procedures, nuclear fuel operators have it pretty good."

The doctor didn't respond. A sudden, horrible thought invaded Nic's consciousness. Was her accident and the recent events in his life somehow linked? Asking the health professional resulted in the doctor looking away but quickly recovering. Nic was certain the entire story would not be revealed. In the end, he realized only one question really mattered.

"Is she going to be all right?" It was the doctor's turn to consider the words.

"Define 'all right.'"

"You know, will she be able to come home and do the things she used to?"

"At present, that is uncertain. In the current acute period, she will remain on life support. She will be evaluated periodically. The next stage will be to determine if she will be able to walk again."

The words shocked Nic. *Life support, walk again? Just how serious were the injuries?* "I would like to see her."

"It is unadvisable given her current condition."

Nic had had enough. The antiseptic treatment and businesslike environment infuriated him. "I demand to see her. She's my mom."

The holo, who had been listening to the entire conversation, chimed in. "That is not possible. As a minor, you do not have those rights. It is advised you return home, as you are now informed of her situation. She is now in the capable care of the State. You will be informed when it is possible to return."

Nic decided he hated holos. They had brought to him nothing but trouble.

Chapter Twenty-Two

With his mom in the hospital, Nic developed a routine where he spent as little time as possible at home. The empty apartment left him feeling isolated. When returning home from school, he would check the Screen. Always, nothing. An update would be helpful, even if it meant his mom still needed to stay at the hospital. Apparently, the staff there didn't find it important enough to give him this occasional courtesy.

The lack of time at home forced him to do other things. At first he went for long walks, trying to collect his thoughts. He didn't know how to approach his friends about his mom. At some point they would find out. Visiting his home would sooner or later reveal her lengthy absence. Since Nic wasn't at home much, however, this didn't concern him.

Not having the opportunity at lunch to talk with Willow bothered him. She often chose to sit with some of the students from her judo club. He was envious when she was with other boys,

---

Nic Rocke   Marc Sherrod   ~ 133 ~

and felt a deep sense of hurt when he saw her laughing and seeming to enjoy herself around them. Nic noticed curves to her body. She looked stronger now. *How different she is. No longer shy.*

A couple of times, it felt as if she might be looking in his direction. The feeling was similar to when he had first met her. When turning around to check, he would find either she was not there or was engaged in discussion with someone else. Nic felt his emotions were toying with him. Annoyed, he would brush past her without saying anything. Part of him realized he was being selfish. *I have no right to stop her. If she wants to make new friends, then that's her own business.* With his mom in the hospital, more than ever he craved her presence. *Things are different now though. Something has changed between us.*

She seemed to be moving forward. He was angry at her for doing so, but also angry at himself for knowing that growing like this was good for her, but still wanting her to spend time exclusively with him. The emotional drain started taking its toll. His feelings for Willow were very confusing.

Several days into his walks, Nic decided to spend his time more productively. He wasn't able to resolve his feelings about Willow. *I remember when we walked together here... it seems so long ago.* At home, the silence of the Screen mocked him. *Nothing, again. No calls. Why do I even bother checking? I have to do something.*

Extra training was held every day after the regular basebasket practices. Nic originally thought these were for the more senior players, but Smith informed him anyone could go to them. He still felt intimidated, as he heard that many players, except the elite, wouldn't go. It was time for him to see if this was true.

No one seemed particularly surprised as he entered the workout room from the courts. A few of the players were already setting the adjustments on the lifting bars to the desired weight levels. Nic had never lifted and wasn't sure what to do. The bars looked simple enough, but he knew he would need to learn more before trying it on his own.

"Ever try one?" The question came from his left side. The coach had entered and was looking across the room to see who had come to the training session. Nic shook his head. "It's pretty simple, just don't set the weight too high or you'll rip your arms off." Nic gave a look that was part alarm and part disbelief. "Everyone falls for that one. Seriously though, you need to find the right level. Too heavy and you could hurt yourself. Too light and you'll become bored." The coach picked a bar up and flipped a few switches. "Hmm, this should do it. Give it a try."

Nic picked up the bar carefully. The metal was light to the touch at first, but as he pulled with more strength, it resisted him. He tried several standing curls, each time pulling with force. The bar responded, making it difficult after a set of ten curls for him to do any more. Gently he put down the bar and massaged his tired muscles.

"How was it?" the coach asked.

"Good. It didn't take much though. I'm tired."

"You'll get used to it. Repeat that every other day. Once you get a full set down we'll look at working you up to two. Now, let's start on your calves."

Later that night at home, Nic imagined himself as a bowl of spaghetti. His muscles felt loose, his energy drained for the day. As tired as he was, it felt good. He slept soundly, his fears and concerns momentarily shelved.

****

As the coach had promised, his workout regimen increased. The first two weeks were difficult as his strained body responded wearily to the increased stress placed on it. Several times however, he believed he was making progress. The workouts allowed him to sleep better, resulting in greater alertness in the morning. While he still worried about both Willow and his mom, the exercise seemed to remove an edge which had been beating him down before.

The coach had Nic play in the following two games. Nic was asked to come in both times late in the game. While the mound wasn't as intimidating as the first time, he still felt a thrill walking onto the court with all eyes on him. Both times he looked for Willow in the stands, even though he didn't expect to see her. She wasn't at either game.

His team won both games. He didn't play a major role in the first, but neither did he make the crowd uneasy. His teammates seemed to be playing exceptionally well fielding for the day, making the three hits he gave up a minor issue. For the second game, he pitched well; allowing only one hit over two innings. Nic's confidence soared. In the hallways at school, some of his teammates would go out of their way to come over and talk to him. The attention felt good. Nic ran into Smith in the hallway at lunch the day before the next game.

"Fourth game coming up," Smith said, grinning.

Nic realized Smith's smile was in some way different. Not malicious, but hiding something. "Yeah. Who's starting?"

Smith headed off, chuckling. "You'll see."

The coach informed Nic he would be playing in his fourth game. He expected to play again in the latter part of the match. When Nic checked the lineup, he was shocked. He was listed as the starting pitcher. Visions of his first outing flooded back. The queasiness he had experienced back then also returned. Nic wanted to head to the toilet and vomit.

Keeping busy warming up on the practice mound did little to occupy his mind. The thrill which he had learned to keep under control became a raging force which squeezed his insides. Several of his throws went wide. Even the catching bot had a hard time fielding his pitches.

Every few minutes he checked the time. The clock on the feedback screen seemed to be moving slower than usual. In past games, the coach would have come over to him by now to discuss how he was feeling. But he was on the far side of the court mentoring some of the batters. More than ever, Nic needed guidance. He realized his mind was tricking him into believing others were purposely avoiding him. The last thing he needed were the conflicting emotions fighting inside himself, one part telling him to pitch well, with the other quickly informing him he was going to fail.

Nic walked to the mound to start the game. He felt shaky. Home plate looked far away. The first batter looked like a monster, perhaps even larger than the Beast. Even from this distance, the player towered, exuding a great sense of confidence. The bat was a tiny toothpick in his hands.

"I'm done for," Nic muttered.

The first two pitches were low, as called for by the catcher. The batter didn't move at all, unnerving Nic. On the third pitch, Nic lost some control and sent the cyber-ball several inches higher than expected. The monster took advantage of the mistake and sent the throw spinning high through the court. Outfielders had no chance to catch the blast. It entered the home run hole perfectly; the force sending a resounding clang throughout the crowd. An awkward silence ensued as the player slowly rounded the four bases and headed home. Nic could hear each thud of the player's steps, one after another, demonstrating his sheer strength and confidence.

Disaster continued for the remainder of Nic's time on the mound. The next three batters were all able to hit safely, resulting in two more runs. Nic had yet to produce an out, let alone a strike. The anger from the catcher was clear on the boy's face through his protective mask. Nic had no control over his pitches.

"Time!"

The infielders all gathered with the coach at the mound.

"Just what kind of crap are you throwing?" the catcher screamed at Nic. "The last four haven't been near what I'm calling!"

"Settle down, Johnson," the coach reprimanded. "What's going on, son?"

Nic looked onward. He felt terrible, wanting to run away from this miserable place. All eyes were on him; a thousand, hostile stares glaring at him. The truth was out before he could stop it. "I can't do it," Nic muttered.

For several seconds, no one said anything.

"Okay. Sorry son, day's over for you." The coach extended his hand, waiting for the cyber-ball. Nic felt heavily stung as he handed it over. The ceremonial handing over of the ball, letting the entire crowd know he was being replaced, was deeply humiliating. Nic walked to the bullpen. He felt a surreal sense of detachment as if he were witnessing someone else from a distance moving away in defeat, pretending he was watching a movie.

The loss was a blow to Nic's confidence. He couldn't help but feel responsible. The relief pitchers worked hard to undo the damage, but it was too great. While his teammates didn't outwardly blame him, he could see disappointment in their eyes.

As in the past, Nic scanned the crowds. He didn't expect to see Willow; but still, he hoped. He desperately needed to find something, anything, of comfort. Then, a quick movement on the left side of the bleachers caught his eye. A girl with Willow's height and build was running through the crowd. He couldn't see her face, as she was turned towards the exit. Several angry fans yelling at one another obscured his view. When they settled down and started to move away, the girl was gone.

At home on the couch, Nic reviewed the game. The solo home run shot wouldn't leave his mind. Again and again, he saw the cyber-ball lifting high into the sky, only to come down each time into the home run hole. The details were clear; desperate outfielders reaching vainly for the ball, the pregnant silence as the crowd waited for the inevitable score, several of the lights on the scoreboard needing replacement as they winked on and off. No matter how hard he tried, he couldn't erase the image.

His obsessive thoughts were broken by the Screen's light. The blinking red light informed him a priority call had come through. As before, a soulless holo had left a message. Nic wondered if it to be the same one who had contacted him before.

"Rocke, Nic," it began. *Do all the medical holos use last names first?*

"How is she?" Nic asked, hesitantly. He braced himself for bad news.

"Improving." The holo went on to use vocabulary similar to Nic's experience with his bruised eye and the home doctor a few months ago. Though he could understand little of the detail, the overall impression was that his mom was much better. His mom could be expected back home within two weeks. She wouldn't be able to work, at least for the near future, and she would require daily care. Bots would be available, if the family could afford them, to help with her recovery, otherwise the family would need to find other means.

Nic digested the information. *Mom is better, but she'll need a lot of help.* His relationship with Willow was uncertain as he doubted if they were even friends anymore. He had just embarrassed himself with his pitching in front of several hundred people. *There's no choice. I hate this situation. I will do anything to get out of this mess.*

Chapter Twenty-Three

"You sure are putting in a lot of practice," Smith commented. Nic responded with another fastball. He had been working over the last several weeks to perfect the pitch. It wasn't where he wanted it to be. The feedback screen still showed several red comments. Some of them seemed to contradict one another. "Just don't wear yourself out. Everyone else left an hour ago. The security bots will be here soon."

For every night over the last week, the bots told Nic the school was closed and that it was time to head home. Life had become a routine of hard work. Early mornings and late evenings were concentrations on practice.

"Unbelievable," Michael mentioned one night after catching a fastball from Nic.

"What?" Nic expected criticism from his friend.

"How you have changed."

"That bad, huh."

"No. The opposite. It's like looking at two different people. You've changed, Nic. Yeah, you had a bad night the last game. But you're getting better. Seems like you have been playing this game for years."

****

The hospital delivered his mom to their apartment on a Friday afternoon. She was encased in a cylinder which resembled a coffin more than anything else. A single, tiny window directly over her head allowed him to peer inside. Nic didn't recognize her. He pretended it was all of the cables getting in the way, but he realized after some reflection that he simply couldn't identify her facial features. The reconstructive surgery had greatly changed her appearance.

Lights on the outside of the case indicated her present condition. A hospital bot accompanied his mom to inform Nic of the operation of the cylinder and what to do in case of emergency. She was expected to emerge within a week.

Chapter Twenty-Four

Nic made the starting pitcher rotation. The game after next was his chance for redemption. He promised to himself that he would be ready.

At school, he thought on two occasions that Willow was looking in his direction. He noticed she was not participating in the conversations with her friends, but rather looked past them in his direction as if concentrating on something. *I need to go see her. Maybe she's thinking the same thing. But what if I'm wrong? If she rejects me... no, it would be too painful.* He headed to class without saying anything, brushing by her in a hurry as he had done so many times recently. Nic made contact, his arm lightly touching hers. There was something different about Willow now. Instead of recoiling, her arm pushed back, searching, seeking. The inner strength amazed Nic. Caught off guard, he continued, ignoring her.

On the day of the game, he felt no fluttering in his stomach. Determination to do well, anger at all of the issues he had had to face recently and frustration regarding his situation with Willow all combined to steel him for the competition. He approached the mound with a confidence he hadn't felt before.

His fastball was in top form. The first several batters couldn't touch it. Nic's determination ignited the other players. His teammates swooped in to field the cyber-ball well the few times the batters connected. At the end of the fifth inning, the game was still scoreless. The other pitcher was also doing well. Nic knew the duel would come down to the last inning. He wasn't surprised. His arm ached horribly but he battled on. Twice his coach had visited the mound to discuss bringing in relief, but on both occasions, Nic refused.

"Alright son," the coach commented several times. "Keep taking 'em out."

Nic's team had managed to score at the end of the 8th and was now up by a run. It was up to him to stop the other team. The lead's slim margin allowed for no error. As the game progressed, the crowd became enchanted. Between innings, Nic could hear his name called several times from the stands. The words encouraged him to continue.

There was little left to his throws, but his will carried Nic forward. He gave up a hit but also struck one out. The next batter hit deep. Visions of the home run hole ran through Nic's mind and he gritted his teeth. One of the outfielders snatched the ball from a certain score. The replays showed an incredible catch. Nic had never seen this player jump so high. Inspired, he returned to the mound.

The final batter was the other team's best. He had hit twice safely today. Scoring would send the game into extra innings, or it could mean a loss. *This cannot happen.*

With a full count of theee balls and two strikes, Nic threw his next pitch with everything he had left in him. He thought of his dad and those summer days so long ago and of his mom still recovering. The image of the Beast and his adventure to the suburbs flashed across his mind. As he let go of the cyber-ball he pictured Willow, expressionless, looking in his direction.

The batter swung and missed the ball. Nic slumped to the ground, exhausted. The crowd erupted and broke onto the court, surrounding him, calling out his name. Teammates propped him up and carried him around the infield.

As before, he noticed a girl running from the stands to the exit. The blonde hair this time was unmistakable. He wouldn't let her get away this time. "Willow!" he screamed. The form slowed but continued at an unsteady pace. "No, don't go. I need you." Nic managed to break away from his teammates and run towards the girl. He fell twice but got back up. As he reached her, Willow turned around, tears streaming from her eyes. He had never imagined her face so beautiful.

"Oh Nic," she managed as she wrapped her arms around his form. "I thought you didn't want to talk with me anymore."

"I thought the same about you. Your new club and friends."

"Let's not let this happen again. Okay?" Willow looked up expectantly.

"I promise."

Someone in the crowd was taking pictures of them and asking questions of the teammates about Willow. Nic didn't care. It felt good to hold her again.

Nic Rocke Marc Sherrod

Chapter Twenty-Five

Nic expected the call to be from Conner at this time of the evening. Conner always called right after dinner. He probably wanted to talk about the summer and all the great plans he had. Recently, this was all he would discuss with his friends. He was surprised instead to see a middle-aged man with a serious expression appear on the Screen. A beaming smile replaced the concerned look when he recognized Nic standing in front of the Screen.

"Nic! Good to see you. I'm Mr. Smith. Your coach has said a lot of good things about you; and he should have. What a fine performance, good pitching. I saw it all." The man spoke at several decibel levels higher than was needed. The noise brought his mom hobbling into the room.

"Oh, hello there. You must be Mrs. Rocke. Great athlete, your son. As I just mentioned to him, I'm Mr. Smith. Let me get to the point since the two of you are in front of me at the same time. Always easier that way."

The man paused for effect with a toothy smile plastered across his face. He reminded Nic of a hover-car salesman Nic once saw advertising on the Screen. When neither Nic nor his mom said anything, the man continued. "Your performance was so good, such a capstone to an excellent season, we just couldn't resist. I would like to offer you a chance to come play for us. It's the big time, Nic."

"What?" Both Nic and his mom simultaneously shouted and looked at each other, puzzled.

"That's right. College ball, offered exclusively to you. We would like you to come and play for the school. We hope you'll join us."

The man's offer struck Nic. Apparently his mom got it now, too. Her eyes seemed to be swimming. "Well, we certainly will consider your generous offer. What have you got to say, honey?"

All eyes focused on him. Nic felt a tremendous weight come crashing down. "Yeah. This is great."

His mom and the recruiter continued to exchange a few more pleasantries. The recruiter mentioned several times what a wonderful addition Nic would make. After the call ended, his mom turned to face him. "You could have shown a little more appreciation, Nic."

"Mom, I don't want to go."

Nic's mom considered what he said. "It's a lot to think about, I know. Sleep on it, we'll talk tomorrow."

Nic didn't sleep that night. He thought incessantly about the decision and what he would have to give up. Nic was tired of moving every few years.

The next day things were no better. When he mentioned again his reluctance to leave, his mom was about to reply but instead walked over to the couch and sat down. He couldn't remember her ever looking this tired. Two days ago she had come out of the capsule but was still very shaky. She stared at the Screen but said nothing. Nic felt compelled to justify himself.

"Look, I get it; it would be a great opportunity for me. This kind of thing doesn't happen very often, I know. One of Michael's hover-soccer teammates got accepted and the school made a big deal about it. No doubt I will get a parade myself next week."

"Do you know what happens if you don't go, Nic?" His mom looked at him with teary eyes. He felt he was greatly disappointing her. "This." She looked around the room, and then held up her tattered sleepwear by the shoulder with pinched fingers. "And this." She pointed at the walls of the dingy apartment. Nic recalled the times he had asked him mom to change some of the things in their apartment. They never had been able to upgrade anything. "You shouldn't wind up like this. You are being given a way out."

"I said I know, Mom. This is a hard decision."

"Your first difficult one, Nic. There will be more. You're growing up." She smiled slightly and wiped away a tear from the corner of her eye. "I also have a difficult decision I have had to make, honey. I was going to wait until next week when school is out. With the news today, now is a better time to tell you." Nic froze. Mom's news was always big. "I can't work anymore. Later this summer I'll be heading back east. My cousins have agreed to take me in."

Nic Rocke   Marc Sherrod

Chapter Twenty-Six

The library seemed peaceful at dusk. Its monolithic shape, usually imposing, was dwarfed by the setting sun. Bathed in the sun's rays, its surface rippled with reflected light, giving the appearance of a skin decorated by small diamonds. Nic had never viewed the building in this way. It was hard to believe the experience with the strange holo all those months ago had occurred here. He returned home from the walk after reflecting on all of the recent events.

"Why would they have an interest in me?" he had asked his mom. "There are many out there better than I am."

"Sometimes natural talent shows up late," him mom replied with a hopeful voice.

Nic realized he would have to give her more in order to convince her that the situation was strange. "Look here," he pointed to the Screen, "All the sports programs are listed. No basebasket."

His mom thoroughly examined the site, asking Nic to scroll several times. A puzzled look crossed her face. She sat motionless for a few seconds but a knowing look finally crossed her face. "Basebasket is not a heavily funded sport, at least not like the martial arts are. That might be the reason."

For the rest of the conversation, whatever he brought up, she refuted. Nic stormed out of the apartment.

****

It was unfair to her, he now realized, to have acted that way. She tried to provide for them for nearly a year now, in this new location. The incident at the plant wasn't her fault. He knew she needed help, and heading back east was the best thing for her. This wasn't a time to be selfish. His going away to school would unburden her.

Nic wished he could go back in time and undo his violent tantrum as he stormed out the door. Slamming his fist into the wall, he was sure he caused some damage before leaving. The slight cracking sound of the wall and a sore hand were proof. A tired feeling now plagued him. Blind rage had been replaced with regret at his departure. The carousel of emotions continued. Skepticism followed. He had done well in his last game, but there were plenty of more experienced players who excelled at the game much better than he did. *Why am I being given this opportunity?* Sorrow was next, imagining his mom alone in their apartment and the turmoil this sudden change was causing her. Ever since he could remember, she had never been able to find time to slow down and enjoy anything. Moves and work were her sole existence.

Nic felt emotionally spent. He walked by the school, realizing next year he wouldn't be back with his friends. Later in the summer, students would complain about having to come back, but that would wear off quickly on the first day when friends met again and discussed all of the great experiences they had over the summer. Even the school now seemed in some way different. His experiences on the team, the talks in the lunchroom, and even the encounters with the Beast were all now another person's experiences. Nic realized he was emotionally distancing himself, and despite his best efforts, found he was along for the ride. He wasn't able to stop the door from closing.

Tomorrow he would have to tell all of them the news. He would miss his friends as he realized some day they too, would fade into the background. A few Screen calls would artificially extend their friendship, but at some point the talks would end. His experience with Tommy almost a year ago had demonstrated that. *I can accept this. But how do I tell Willow? I have no idea what to say.*

****

Early in the day, Nic realized he had been avoiding Willow. He prolonged minute tasks in class and created extra work for himself, just to keep busy. No matter what he did, from the back of his mind was the thought that nagged at him. *I have to face her before the end of the day.*

The cafeteria would have been the ideal location to talk, had it not been for the throng of students congratulating him on being recruited. He regretted informing Conner and Michael of the news when he arrived at school. They meant well, but word traveling around the school fast was an afterthought for Nic. The sheer number who knew suggested to him that there would have been no possibility of Willow not having heard the news, as well. Then he found out she hadn't been seen since the first hour of class. *I can't find her anywhere. Did she hear about me and leave?* During chemistry class he dropped a tube of some type of acid that burned one of the student's mini-Screens. *I can't do anything right today!* When school was over for the day, he darted out the door, leaving classmates wondering about his obvious anxiety.

He ran all the way to her home. The last mile or so was difficult but he managed to keep going. There were several times he almost ran into people emerging from office building. On one occasion a bot guiding a lev car with supplies nearly knocked him down. He staggered for a moment at the impact, and although he twisted his left ankle, he limped the last mile. Out of breath, he reached Willow's front door. Expecting that he would need to call her several times before she would answer, he was instead alarmed to find the door slightly open. Thoughts of another home invasion flooded his mind.

Cautiously, he crept through the entranceway, hoping to catch anyone who had come through. This time, he was confident he could face the unwelcome intruders. Surprisingly, the apartment wasn't in a state of upheaval. In fact, there was little left to disturb. Almost all of the contents of the home had disappeared. Anyone coming in would have thought no one lived here.

Nic was drawn to the center of the room where he found a picture with an envelope lying next to it. The picture was of Nic and Willow the night of the basebasket victory. He'd forgotten she had taken it. She looked the happiest he'd ever seen her. The envelope lay ominously to the side. As he turned it over, he wasn't sure how to feel as he recognized her handwriting with his name on the front.

Dear Nic,

I remember the first day of class when you came in. The Beast was hard on you but you stood up to him. I knew then that there was something special about you.

It was hard for me to approach you. Sometimes I would watch you, see what you were doing. If you only knew, you might have thought some creepy girl was following you around! When we got to work together on the project for school, I was so happy. You became a person I could trust.

I was so scared when we went to the Butler house. You were with me though, so I knew things would turn out. The Guardians were horrible; I thought they would find us. But somehow I knew, even if they did, we'd make it. Nic, only my parents have ever made me feel so safe.

At the game, when someone asked if I was your girlfriend, I didn't know what to say. This is hard for me to write about, Nic. I was happy then. I hope you feel the same.

Something has happened, Nic. I don't know everything, but it's about my parents. Someone has told me more about them. It's the truth Nic, only someone who really knew them could have said the things he did. I have to find out what happened to them.

I'm proud of you, Nic. Sounds like what a parent would say, but I am. It must have been hard to move here and face all these things. You have changed my life.

I need to go away, maybe for a little while, maybe for longer. I can't ask you to come with me, that would be unfair. You have college. I know you'll do well.

I hope you understand, Nic. I know I will miss you.

~W

Nic read through the letter several times, but with each reading he still felt numb. He couldn't accept this turn of events. As evening approached and the sky grew dim, Nic picked up both the picture and the letter, and headed home.

****

The few weeks leading up to leaving for college passed for Nic as if he were in a dream. He felt distant, detached, as if he were watching his life from another person's point of view. It was difficult for him to accept that Willow was gone. He had finally come to the realization she had become more than a friend to him. On several occasions, Conner had tried to approach him about the issue but he waived his friend away. Nic simply was in no mood to talk about what had happened.

During the final day of school, a number of students wished him well. Nic muttered empty thanks and longed for the day to be over. Among the joyous celebrating of the students and discussions regarding the big plans everyone had for the summer, Nic felt alone. A final Screen call to friends confirmed his isolation. They had all accepted his departure and were moving on with their lives. Michael even left during the conversation to attend some type of training and Bobby didn't even look up. Conner mentioned that Nic should stay in touch, but he wondered if he really meant it. The only person who showed any emotion for the changes taking place was his mom. An incredible burden had been lifted from her. She

Nic Rocke Marc Sherrod

didn't slump forward any longer, but instead worked with a level of enthusiasm he hadn't seen since they first moved to the apartment. He couldn't help but feel he had added to her difficulties these last few years.

****

The day arrived for him to leave for the new school. Before Willow's departure, he had planned to walk around the city to visit some of the places that held key memories for him. Since her leaving, little of his home held any value for him now.

Mechanically, he packed his bags and left the apartment, preferring not to look back. This place, to Nic, was now just one more item on a long list of places he had lived which no longer meant anything to him.

Nic Rocke

Marc Sherrod

Chapter Twenty-Seven

Nic had never been to Texas. Prior to his departure, an odd assortment of images assembled in his mind to paint a strange impression; the Cowboys and cattle he read about when he was younger. Apparently, it used to be home to oil, used before the country accepted both solar and mag-lev as more efficient and cleaner energy sources. He imagined oil wells dotting the skyline as relics of the past as his train pushed its way through the barren wastelands of Texas, but was disappointed when he found none.

The trip gave him time to think about the direction his life was headed. *Mom heading back east is good. I didn't like my cousins growing up, but they've changed as they've grown older. They will take good care of her.* He looked forward to the new school, if only because he could concentrate on basebasket. *I can forget the past. There will be nothing familiar.*

Always clawing at the back of his mind were his memories of Willow. No matter how hard he tried, he couldn't suppress them.

Nic felt betrayed, not by Willow, but rather by his own anger and doubt. They led him to drift away from her. *Would things be different now if I had paid more attention to her at school after we started going our separate ways? Her presence at the games meant she must have had some feelings for me too, didn't it? Does she think about me at all now? I can't be upset with her... this is so confusing. I hope Willow's safe, wherever she is.*

The barren landscape seemed to reflect his thoughts. The train stopped several times to pick up more students. He was surprised at the condition of the train. It was old and shook heavily at times. *Couldn't they have at least brought me by something a little more modern? I don't think it's even linked to the system. Not even a mag-lev. Almost like they want me brought in secret.* Several new riders tried to engage him in small talk, but moved on when he didn't respond.

Nic finally fell asleep, and was startled when the announcement was made to signal that they were close to the college. The train decelerated with force, causing the gawkers to squeal with excitement at the power of the vehicle. Old buildings came into view, their exteriors populated by individuals running in groups. Several of the structures were stark and bare, little more than brick and girders. A team leader seemed to be at the head of every column of runners, clearly barking out instructions, to which each individual complied. Nic guessed this must be a military training camp of some type on the outskirts of the college. When the train stopped, he assumed it would be to pick up more passengers on the route into the college. The sudden surge of his fellow riders grabbing bags and other belongings confused him.

"Why is everyone leaving?" Nic asked to no one in particular.

A teen boy about the same age looked back at him and answered. "We have arrived," came the reply, with a matter-of-fact tone.

"That, out there. That's it?" Nic asked, showing his surprise.

"Yeah, what did you think; that you were going to some elite college or something?" The other smirked, rolled his eyes and shook his head.

Nic gathered his stuff and headed out with the herd. The train moved on, leaving an eerie silence. The buildings he witnessed from the window of the train were the only ones in sight. *Something's not right. Have I been tricked? If this isn't a college with a basebasket team, then what exactly is it?*

The group continued to move forward towards the dilapidated structures. A person not much older than them was waiting for the group to approach. He had a stern, disapproving look. Instinctively, they formed a circle around him. Nic immediately distrusted him.

"Welcome to your first day of training. I'm Jones. We don't use our first names here as it compromises security. You there, pay attention." Someone shuffled to Nic's right and looked up, clearly embarrassed. The boy had been fidgeting with one of his bags. "You come from all walks of life. It does not matter what you once were. That's no longer. Each of you is a *KAY-det* now. That is how you say it, emphasis on the first syllable. *KAY-det.* Got it?" The boy looked around at the group. "Not a rhetorical question people. I will ask again. Do you understand?" Several murmured in the crowd. "I can wait here all day." All in the group screamed a strong response. "Good. That's how it works here, see? I say something, you obey. There are just two types here, those who speak, and those who listen. You are in the second group. If you perform well, you might be asked to join the first. Looking at this sorry bunch, I doubt there will be many who move up; if any."

Nic immediately disliked this older boy. A few of the basebasket players had the same condescending attitude. After he proved himself, their behavior towards him changed. He felt, however, this one would take much more convincing.

"You will walk with me to those buildings over there for processing. You will be catalogued and assigned to a team. The team will become your existence. Without them, you are meaningless. You will come to accept this way of life or you will cease. It's as simple as that."

As the group moved towards the buildings, Nic approached Jones. He was unsure what Jones would say but he figured it was okay to ask. "Excuse me. I was told I was coming to be part of a basebasket team. I don't see a gym over there."

Jones chuckled for a few seconds and then replied. "Used the sports team hook on you, did they? Smith, he's the best one. Comes up with the most convincing stories. Haven't heard that one in a while."

"So, there's no team?"

"No, there is not, *kay-det* Rocke. No team, no gym. Nothing. Just a lot of hard work as part of your team. Get it?" He wondered how Jones already knew his name. As if reading his mind, Jones continued. "If you think you can run away from here, forget it. One hundred miles to the nearest town. No exaggeration, almost to the foot. Even if you do get that far, they'll just send you back. I know... I've tried."

****

Nic didn't sleep well the first night. Drifting in and out of consciousness, he imagined running through the desert to leave this dreadful place. Each time, Jones caught him at the last moment and dragged him back. The destination in his dreams was not clear, but he was certain anywhere was better than this place.

Nic was angry. He had been duped. After all he had been through the last few months, this was too much. It didn't matter what Jones said. He got out of bed and looked around. Everyone was in deep sleep, exhausted from the day's events. Gathering several bottles of water and other provisions, he crept cautiously towards the exit. At the door, he looked out, scanning the vacant terrain in the distance. *Anything is better than staying in this place, even if I don't make it.*

It almost seemed too easy. *Is there no security?* As he continued across the compound, Nic thought he heard noises behind some of the buildings. He dismissed them as paranoid thoughts and kept moving. Several minutes later, he reached the front gate. It was unguarded. Nic thought he had seen two senior cadets yesterday acting as sentries. *Too easy,* he thought again. Not wanting to wait around to find out why, he ran through the gate, trying to put as much distance between himself and the compound.

A rushing sound emerged from behind and Nic was swept off the ground. Something smashed into his head, leaving him senseless. As he recovered, he looked up to see Jones leering down at him. The senior cadet lowered a weapon which resembled a large bamboo sword. "Thought so," the older cadet said in a calm monotone. "I can always pick out the trouble makers. Get back to your barracks. Now." On his way back, Nic decided he hated Jones.

****

The next morning, Nic was awakened by a blast of music which echoed throughout the base. The music sounded familiar; perhaps he'd heard it from one of the movies he'd watched about soldiers training for one of the world wars.

Jones came rushing into the barracks screaming vulgarities and pushing around the new arrivals. One individual was forcibly removed from his bed. The short, dumpy boy somehow slept through the blaring noise from outside. He found himself pushed to the floor. When he had fully awakened, the senior had assembled everyone else into line and was barking at the latecomer to step it up or else face something called "quarantine." Nic didn't like the sound of that. He felt sorry for the kid who looked helpless in this strange new environment.

For the next several hours, the group ran. There were a few rest stops providing barely enough water to gulp before the team was ordered to proceed to the next point. Several in the group fell out of line, gasping for air. Jones ordered the group to stop, wheeled around, and raced to where the three were lying on the ground. "Quarantine, all of you," he began. "The cart will be here shortly to pick you up."

The group continued to the last stopping point. Nic imagined they were miles from the camp. They entered a woods lightly populated with various types of underbrush and floral growth. Everything here seemed choked, cut off from proper resources. Nic imagined the tree roots battling a vicious war underground for the little water in the land.

From a thicket, emerged a tall, slender man. He looked weathered, like his surroundings, but Nic detected an underlying, incalculable strength. His wiry form approached the group. It was hard to read his facial expression, hidden behind a face full of bristles. The dirty white beard parted and the man spoke in a slow, authoritative voice. A much younger man, tanned with chiseled features, accompanied him.

"I'm One," he said. "Your base leader. You are new to this place, and therefore will require proper acclimation. Every day you will run, as a team. You will learn to think, as a team. You will dine and rest, all as a team. Your individual consciousness will became part of a greater whole. There will be moments you will resist. This is part of the natural process. In time, you will find however, great strength in this way of life. You will find satisfaction in what you and your team can accomplish. You will realize the value of persistence against odds stacked heavily against you." One turned away for a moment, smiled and nodded his head as if recalling an old memory. He faced the crowd again.

"Some of you were brought here with the upfront understanding of what you would face. Others were brought here by what you might think were less than scrupulous means. No matter. You have all been hand-picked because you demonstrated to someone out there in the greater world that you have something of value. If you feel you have been tricked, think about this. Would you rather still be there, in your previous existence?" His eyes narrowed and focused, turning his head slowly and coming to stop in Nic's direction. "Oh yes, we have done our own homework well. We know who you are and what you were facing."

Nic wanted to respond, but felt it prudent not to do so. Unlike Jones, there was something to this leader called One. They had been checking him out for some time. The experiences with basebasket must have been some kind of test. Nic was still very angry about being tricked, but he knew nothing could be done right now. Clearly, some of the others had been tricked as well. The expression was clear on their faces. Nic wondered how they would deal with this.

On the return run back, several other cadets fell out of line and were quarantined immediately. Nic contemplated One's comments. *I can't believe I was tricked so easily! But One is right. I have nothing back home. Home. This place is now where I live. Someone, or maybe even more than a single person, selected me. Who is Smith and how could Coach have been tricked so easily into recommending me for a school which really isn't one? Perhaps some of his players from earlier years had showed up here, too.*

****

Jones was in fine form back at the camp. The senior seemed to enjoy with zest ordering others around, occasionally pushing them down, as well. Several times, Nic wanted to protest at the treatment of his fellow cadets but he held his tongue each time. The wrath of Jones could easily come to him and weave a path of misery for Nic, if Jones perceived Nic to be challenging his authority.

With no time to rest, everyone was assigned responsibilities. Most of the work was drudgery. The senseless movement of heavy objects to various locations wearied his group, but no one said anything. All were afraid the verbal lashing they might receive, or worse. The kid who overslept earlier in the day dropped several buckets of water, earning Jones' anger. He banished the unfortunate boy, telling him to find another group and stay out of sight, otherwise he would be quarantined. The kid roamed around aimlessly, his short, squat legs carrying him in different directions. Nic took pity on him. "Over here," he called out. The other boy turned and headed in Nic's direction.

Thick, round glasses covered much of the boy's face. His eyes appeared as giant saucers. Nic could see details in the boy's eyes given the exaggerated appearance. Several veins stood out, the deep red in contrast with the white surrounding. His upper lip appeared puffy. The boy still continued to whimper as he approached. "Take it easy," Nic said. "Don't let him get to you. He just enjoys doing that to us."

"He's a meanie," the short boy blurted.

"Yeah, I guess you could call him that." Nic paused and looked the boy up and down. "So what's your name?"

"Dodi."

"Is that your first or last name?"

"Ssh!" The boy looked serious; his saucer eyes loomed even larger. "Don't you know, only use your first name here." The boy drew close and whispered in Nic's ear. "It's for security reasons."

"Hmmm. I think we are only supposed to use our last names."

"Oh darn! I knew I didn't get it right." The boy continued to tremble, looking fearfully around him.

"It's okay." Nic tried to soothe the boy, but he continued to twitch, clearly agitated at his failure to follow the rule. "I'm Rocke. Why don't you come over and help me move these containers."

Nic spent the remainder of the day helping Dodi follow simple rules. Whatever he did, the younger boy mimicked. Processes requiring more than three steps were impossible for the boy. Nic wondered why he was at this type of camp. Keeping an eye on Dodi became a full-time job. Nic knew he didn't owe him anything, but he felt sorry for the boy. Being relocated to this barren place was difficult for even the hardiest of the cadets. It must be nightmarish for a kid as young and as small as Dodi to be uprooted from wherever he came from and planted in this abysmal place. He decided to find out more about him. "What do you think about this place?" Nic opened up casually several days after their first meeting.

"Hot, sunny." Came the reply.

"Do you think about home a lot?"

"Home. Yeah. Sometimes."

Even though the answers were short, they were a start. Nic decided the boy was capable, and willing, to reveal more. "It seems we were all brought here for different reasons. I still can't figure out why I'm here. Any reason you know of why you were brought here?"

The unblinking eyes stared vacantly at Nic. "No."

"You can't think of any reason?"

"No."

"Really?"

"No."

The current line of inquiry was going nowhere. Nic realized he would need to take a different approach. "My guess is we all have something to offer. Again, I'm still trying to figure that one out about myself. Maybe you have a skill needed here. Is there something special you can do?"

Nic could see Dodi working hard on this one. His eyes closed for a few seconds and quickly opened. The result, however, was the same. "No. Nothing special."

"What do you like to do?"

"Math. I like math."

The revelation reminded Nic of Willow. He had thought of her fleetingly since his arrival at camp. "Math. That's good. What kind?"

"Any."

"That's a lot to choose from. Let's start simple. Addition; you like that?"

"Yes."

"Can you add in your head?"

"Yes."

"Let's try 47 and 35."

The answer was back from Dodi hardly a second after he had spoken. "82."

"Pretty fast, good job," Nic congratulated. "This next one might take a little longer. 306 and 998."

With the same speed as before, Dodi answered. "1,304."

"Wow. I'm impressed. I bet 1,330,768 and 2,568,435 is an easy one then too," Nic joked.

"3,899,203," came the instant reply.

Nic was astonished. Dodi stood, unblinking, with no expression. The boy's mathematical skills far outweighed anything he had ever seen. It must all be natural, as nano-enhanced genetic engineering had been outlawed decades ago. Little wonder then, why he was here. This skill was a rare gift, and someone had taken notice. Somebody found it extremely valuable.

Chapter Twenty-Eight

As One had promised, Nic and his other team members did everything together. The early mornings and running several miles had become the routine. Fewer individuals fell out of the ranks due to exhaustion. All seemed to be shaping up. Kids who looked rather frail when everyone arrived at the camp now looked wiry and tanned.

One morning, Jones woke everyone with a rattling of a long bamboo sword against the wall. He was dressed in strange armor, his face difficult to see through a metal grating. Several of the cadets looked at one another, wondering about his bizarre appearance. "You are now at a point where we can begin Kendo training," he began. "Before, you were in a sorry shape. Now you are at a point where I can work with you. Follow me."

The group headed in the opposite direction from the path usually taken to begin the daily run. They entered a musty old hall. Nic was certain a storm would easily knock the building down. The floor was covered with small divots. Jones noticed Nic's examination of the ground. He addressed the group. "Many have come through here to practice this ancient art. You see the result of their efforts; there, there, everywhere. They have ground down even the floor with their efforts, generation after generation. People who have gone on to do great things started here. Don't disappoint me."

Jones directed the cadets to select the appropriate armor and bamboo swords. Nic tried several breastplates, known as *do,* but all were too small. He found an older one tucked away further back from the others. It was the right size, but heavily used. Still, it seemed intact, evidence of good craftsmanship. He had better luck with finding both sword and helmet. His sword, or *shinai,* had seen action but was firm. There was no splintering, which would have made the *shinai* worthless. His helmet, or *men,* fit well. There was an ancient odor of stale sweat as he placed it on top of his head. It fit snuggly around him. He wondered how many before him had used this one.

"Discipline and strength, opportunity and patience, attack and defense," Jones said, addressing the crowd. "You will learn the importance of all of these."

Practice with the armor was hard. It was clear the extra bulk encumbered the body, as Nic felt the extra weight press upon him. The *men* made it difficult to breathe as well, even though the front was covered with a metal grating allowing for air to come through. The cadets seemed like clumsy toys at first, wobbling about the floor. Dodi looked ridiculous; Nic could still see his piercing, frightened eyes behind the metal grating. Twice he fell over, sending his *shinai* skittering across the floor. One cadet even laughed at the sight, earning Jones' wrath. After several sessions, Nic still found the practices difficult. Swinging the *shinai* properly to score correct attacks on the opponent was difficult. At times, it appeared Jones' patience was wearing thin, but he continued to train the group through gritted teeth.

Several weeks passed. The days continued to be occupied by physical conditioning. Even those who had been quarantined returned. They were somehow different. Nic was not able to pinpoint the changes, but they were able to keep up. Some seemed confident, motivated. A couple others even seemed happier. *I wonder what happens in the quarantine block of the base camp.* On one occasion, he tried to take a shortcut near the quarantine building in order to be on time for an afternoon run starting from the far side of the camp. The man who stood by One when Nic first met the camp leader, appeared and informed him politely, but firmly, the area was not accessible to cadets outside of quarantine.

The team members weren't allowed to discuss anything while running. The same was true at "lights out," when everyone was expected to hurry up for bed and promptly fall asleep. Jones had barked that discipline and effort were critical in helping them to get fit. One unfortunate person decided he was going to ignore the requirement and tried to talk to another team member in a whispery voice. The other wanted nothing to do with the conversation and rolled over, pretending not to listen. Jones appeared from behind the front door. It didn't matter to him who had initiated the conversation.

"Out, now!" Jones screamed.

Both boys looked terrified. "What? I just want to sleep!" the one boy protested.

"Doesn't matter," Jones replied. "Both of you have broken the rules!" Swooping into the sleeping bay, he plucked both out of bed and dragged them out into the night air for additional "training."

At mealtimes, however, everyone was allowed to talk. Senior students roamed among the tables, a constant reminder to the cadets of their complete immersion in the training routine. Rarely did the seniors intervene in the discussions, even if the conversations were negative about the day's activities. Nic found this level of tolerance on the part of the staff surprising. Staff members were obviously listening to the content of the conversations. Cadets who came to the table tired and unhappy often left after voicing their frustrations in much better spirits. *I wonder if this is intentional. Do they want the cadets to let out whatever is bothering them and to move on?*

Before going to sleep on the night of his one-month anniversary at the camp, Nic reflected on his experience so far. In addition to not revealing first names, individuals were not encouraged to give details of their places of origin. Wang was from out west somewhere. The boy towered above everyone else. It was clear his strength was an asset. He also proved to have an iron will. With a tendency to be short-tempered, Nic thought of him as an explosive, powerful force. He was generally reliable, unless provoked. One of the others on the team discovered arguing with him would result in an inescapable bear hug.

Nic realized Schneider was another story. No one knew anything about his life before coming to the base. He was nondescript. Average size, average height. He was the type of person who blended into the crowd and was forgotten within a short period of time. Like Dodi, he answered in monosyllables. He did exhibit however, a keen observation of the world around him. Schneider seemed to study thoroughly before taking action. Nic was unsure whether to trust this one.

Trenton exuded confidence. Like Schneider, she was keenly aware of her surroundings. When she looked at Nic he felt she was looking through him, probing his thoughts, learning his secrets. She was outspoken, not afraid to express herself. Her presence was immediately noticeable when entering a room. Nic considered her to be beautiful; something which he felt could be dangerous should she learn this about him. He didn't know the reason for feeling this way. She let slip that her first name was Lauren, but Nic concluded it was an intentional mistake; for some purpose she wanted him to know it. He decided it was best to be guarded around her.

The last individual to impress Nic was a prankster. Onizuki had the dubious distinction of being first in the group to be quarantined, falling unconscious on the first day during the run. "Oni," as he liked to be called, which someone had mentioned meant 'troll' in Japanese, had a habit of hiding others' personal belongings, usually at the most unfortunate times. His quick speed and eye for opportunity allowed him to creep stealthily among the other cadets and remove their belongings. Twice Nic had to run without socks, resulting in an irritable chaffing of his feet.

****

Days grew shorter as the team continued to train. One had introduced classroom learning opportunities where the team members would be asked what they knew of historical as well as contemporary events. Much of what Nic had thought to be correct was re-examined. One never suggested right from wrong, preferring to let the cadets arrive at their own conclusions. Old books were used during the sessions, some of such an age they were falling apart and had to be held together with a primitive, sticky substance manufactured somewhere on the base. These were even older than the one hid safely away at home he and Willow used to find out about Butler. Nic marveled at the self-sufficiency of the base. It was cut off from the outside world, but managed to survive despite its lack of modern day advantages.

Nic, on one run, had the opportunity during a rest period to look in a dirty pool of water, revealing its brackish, stagnant contents. He was amazed at the physical changes that had taken place. Looking back at him was a wiser, stronger version of what he used to be. Many times during recent Kendo practice he had been able to score correct hits and was able to defeat his fellow cadets. His face revealed a questioning hunger coupled with a mental confidence. Physically, he was stronger and faster and had learned skills such as climbing and swimming. Nic felt confident; more than ever before.

Chapter Twenty-Nine

Jones continued his reign of terror among the group over the weeks that followed. He was assigned as their permanent senior leader, a role he clearly relished. The move energized him, resulting in more bullying. All despised him.

"I don't care, I would take him out. Just give me a knife."

"Don't be stupid, Oni." Wang replied.

Schneider looked ready to comment but Lauren cut him off. "Why not? A knife's good, but I would like to take Jones out with a *shinai*. Hit to the head with no helmet, he's done."

"Keep it quiet, all of you," Nic responded. "None of you would do any of that and you know it."

****

On several occasions, Nic helped Dodi keep up with the running as the workouts increased in length. The shorter boy would falter, requiring assistance. Otherwise, as with the others, he would face quarantine. Nic urged his group members to help him in order to prevent this. Once Wang even carried Dodi on his shoulders; transforming the wide-eyed genius into a strange, all-seeing tower, his terrified eyes looking all about him from this unusual perch.

"Look at that," one of the boys laughed. "Read about something once called a 'lighthouse.' Here's one!"

"Poor little guy," another mocked. "Hope he doesn't fall off." The boy moved forward to scare Dodi.

"Shut up, all of you!" Jones barked. "Get moving or its extra laps for everyone!"

The runs now included various obstacles in which pairs of cadets had to help each other navigate. A particularly difficult exercise was the "wooden widow." Jones instructed the pairs to create a flimsy, yet navigable bridge from assorted wooden parts in order to traverse a small creek.

"I think I got it, Nic," Oni said.

"Jones is setting us up," Nic replied. "I would wait to learn a little more about where this is going."

"Nah, it's easy. Hey Jones, I mean, uh, Senior *kay-det* Jones, I'll give it a try."

Jones turned his head and smiled. Nic didn't like the look. *A wolf,* he thought. The senior cadet handed the wood politely to Oni. *This is not going to be good.*

After a few minutes, a basic bridge stood. Oni began crossing the bridge, carefully taking steps. Halfway across, he raised his hand in victory. "See Jones, I did it!" Oni cried out.

"Wrong," Jones replied. "I've seen this setup tried before. "Everyone, watch."

As if on cue, the bridge began to wobble. Oni thought the river thin enough to jump the rest of the way but was proved wrong and splashed head-first into the water. The group erupted in laughter until Jones ordered them to be silent.

Team after team failed at the bridge exercise until Jones, exasperated, told all to stand back and watch him do the work. He complained all of them were inept as he built the bridge in half a minute and climbed to the top of the wall.

The pairs then had the opportunity to try again, now that they had been shown the "proper way" to complete the challenge. Nic and Dodi completed their bridge, but the structure didn't impart confidence. A small gust of wind moved the boards.

"Up. Now!" Jones screamed from behind.

Dodi went first, whimpering as he went. Amazingly, he made it to the top, though twice he nearly fell. Nic followed. He tried to step where his partner had, but realized halfway up the bridge wouldn't sustain his weight. Futilely, he clung to one of the boards with both hands. The material snapped in half and Nic fell.

He hit the ground hard, knocking his wind out. Nic fought to get up but needed a few minutes to recover. All other cadets silently urged him to get up through the expressions on their faces. Jones was relentless. He moved to where Nic crouched.

"Everyone, behind me." Jones ordered.

All followed, except Dodi. Wang looked upset, but said nothing. Oni was unusually silent. Schneider and Lauren seemed aloof, but observant. Lauren's eyes seemed to bore through Nic, almost asking him what he would do next. Dodi looked at the group and then at Nic. He waffled, turning one way and then the next. "He really doesn't know what to do, poor kid," Nic realized.

"Just leave him. He is of no use to us," Jones yelled. The small boy stepped towards the group, but then ran to Nic and clung to him, wailing loudly. Jones continued. "I said everyone back in line. You too, little man."

Dodi was pulled up by the arms and thrown to the group. With a last glance at Nic, he offered a weak protest. "But-"

"Silence!"

Nic thought he heard Dodi mention an apology in his direction. The group headed off. Tears streamed down Dodi's face, forming two rivers which circumvented his open, gaping mouth.

****

The silence of the glen was in odd contrast to the earlier battle. Nic moved his legs to make sure they still worked. He felt pain, but was able to stifle it.

He recalled a day many years ago, about a year before his dad left. Some of the boys in the neighborhood had decided they didn't like him and found him alone. Nic had been far from earshot; therefore none of the neighbors heard him screaming out as the bullies continuously punched him. He was in so much pain he was unable to move. The bright sunlight was replaced by an evening cloud cover. It grew dark. In the distance, Nic heard his dad calling for him. As the calling grew closer, he struggled harder to stand. It would be far worse for his dad to find him this way than what the kids had done to him. Nic felt he would let him down if his dad found him like that. His legs gave out as his dad emerged from the trees and found him.

You won't get any better lying there all day." Nic slowly turned his head from facing the ground. Towering above was the man who stood next to One on the day Nic arrived. "Here." The man offered his hand. Nic sat up and took it. He was surprised at the strength of the man as he was lifted up into a standing position. Nic thought he would be sent away to quarantine. "Now, get back to camp and wait for your team to arrive. They need you, even if they don't realize it."

Nic did as he was instructed, relieved at the man's show of mercy. As he ran off, he looked back to thank him, but he had already disappeared.

****

Back at the mess hall, Nic felt alone. It was a different feeling of isolation than when he left home. There, he knew his life was heading in a different direction, an unknown path, leaving all the familiar things he had come to know behind. Now, all that he knew was leaving him. He felt his strength ebbing. What he believed to be a clear direction had become clouded. Doubt entered his mind. He looked around the empty barracks which reflected his inner feelings.

"Nic."

His body jerked as his name was softly spoken behind him. The tone, the whispery quality to the voice, the thrill it caused him to feel.

Willow walked through the doorway, sat down and faced him. A slight smile crossed her face. "I've missed you." Emotions welled up within him. He was unsure whether to scream or hug Willow. *What is happening! Willow... at this camp? How is it possible that she's here, of all places?*

She could see that he didn't know what to say. "I'm sorry I didn't get a chance to say goodbye. It was hard; they asked me to come here and didn't give me a lot of time to think about it. I knew if I asked you, I wouldn't have been able to leave. Kind of funny though, isn't it, we both wind up here?"

Nic struggled to keep quiet. He wanted to ask a thousand questions. As he remained silent taking everything in, she continued.

"It was my math scores. They told me they were interested because of my performance over the last year. I found out, well, that's part of the truth. It's the same with you. Your ability on the court is part of the reason you're here. You had to show the strength to overcome great odds. They look for that in people. The other part is what we went through earlier."

Nic searched his experiences. There were several unusual events over the last year, but one in particular stood out. "It's what happened at Butler's house, isn't it." His comment was more a confession than a question. Nic had wondered what type of attention the experience might have drawn. Now he knew.

"Yes, I think so."

Questions flooded through him as a result of her answer. He barely kept his emotions under control and decided to ask her one at a time. "This really isn't a school. Not the kind you and I are used to."

Willow started several times to respond but stopped each time. She sighed and began again, slowly. "I don't know what it is, either. What I can tell you is that they look for people like us, students mainly, who come across things they're not supposed to find. The holo at the library, our search for Butler. Most people don't look that far into things. We did. Someone noticed us."

Nic recalled the strange man who first gave him the book. He also recalled the Guardians. "More than just someone. Several of them tried to kill us."

"Right. That seems to be the other side. We're in the middle of a battle, Nic. Looks like the side which wants to find out more about what's really going on has recruited us."

Recruited. Nic recalled what the Beast had said about those out there in society placed to stop people like Willow and him. He also remembered his conversations with Conner about students disappearing and not being heard from again. The experiences, this entire strange last year, was starting to make sense. There were still some things that remained a mystery, though. "In your note, you mentioned your parents. How is that wrapped up in this?"

Willow looked away from him and out one of the windows. Nic could see her eyes tearing up and at once regretted his question. "Sorry. I shouldn't have brought that up."

"No. It's okay. I need to face this. I told you earlier that I was born in Valley Creek. That's not all, though. My parents worked out there. I'm still trying to find out what they did, exactly.

They knew Butler, Nic. At least they had met him. One of the instructors here informed me of this."

Nic imagined another key fitting into place and a door opening. Parts of the puzzle were now coming together. "So you trust what the instructor told you."

"Yes, I have to trust them. When I was younger, I could have never understood. Now, it seems a good time to be learning all of this. I'm not the first in my family to come to this school. Nic, my parents were recruited and came here before I was born. They went by different names back then to protect their identities. I think they called themselves Derek and Anne."

There was a moment of silence as Nic considered all Willow had told him. "It's good you have found out something about your parents."

"I haven't told you everything." Willow returned her gaze from the window and looked directly at him. "Nic, your mom was not in an accident. Someone was trying to sidetrack you. People on our side intervened; found her at the plant before it was too late. Otherwise it would have been far worse."

Anger burned deep inside Nic. He had wondered how much of this was actually an "accident" as the hospital staff had informed him. *I will find out who is responsible for all of this!*

Willow saw his expression. "It infuriates me too. I think we'll find the answer to our parents' problems but we have to try together. Okay Nic?"

Nic realized Willow was right. The only way they would get through this was together. "Yes Willow. I promise."

Chapter Thirty

Nic couldn't sleep that night. His thoughts kept twisting, pulling him back from the abyss of unconsciousness. As much as he tried, he couldn't will himself to sleep. There was simply too much to consider. His body screamed for rest, knowing without it, the next day would be difficult to face. Part of him insisted, however, on analyzing all he was experiencing.

I would never have guessed she would show up here. Why hadn't I crossed her path here at the base until now? She simply wandered into the mess hall unannounced. Every day during the team's running I've seen new faces on other teams as they passed on the trails. Given the size of the camp, it's possible she's been here as long as I have, maybe even longer. For her to show up as she has though, is strange. Was this encounter planned? Surely, One must know we went to the same school in the outside world. Was her arrival part of my training? Or am I part of hers?

He also struggled with his feelings for her. Something inside Nic died the day he found her apartment empty. He walled off the feeling, a despair he had never felt before. It was easier to pretend one day she would come back, rather than face the lingering truth that he was likely to never see her again. She remained every day for these last several months as a sign of hope, a tether to the outside world, keeping him sane as he struggled to survive one more day in this barren, foreign world.

Willow was no longer a memory, but rather a part of his life again in this strange land. His feelings for her flooded him, washing away the part within which had died when she left home. His last thought before falling asleep was looking forward to seeing her again tomorrow.

****

Jones announced to the team the next day a new cadet was joining them. When Willow was called, she marched to the front and was introduced. She smiled imperceptibly in Nic's direction. *Her addition to the team is another strange coincidence. Fine. Whatever game is being played out, I'll join.* Nic felt he was being watched. Instinctively he turned to the left to look back. Lauren was staring at him. A barely noticeable look of anger crossed her face. Her eyes then fell on Willow. The anger deepened.

The other cadets, at first, treated Willow indifferently, not knowing the history between she and Nic. They believed his supportive comments of her efforts to be simple encouragement of a new team member, nothing more. Oni cracked a couple of jokes behind her back, receiving a stern look from Nic. Frequent responses like this would raise suspicion Nic realized, therefore he reacted only often enough to send a message to the other team members to treat the new member with the respect she deserved.

The other members of the team, except for Lauren, became supportive, but reserved. On several of the courses, Wang was willing to lend a hand to move some of the larger obstacles when Willow was working with him as a pair to overcome challenges. Even Schneider offered assistance, but unlike Wang, who showed open emotion at both triumph and failure, Schneider was immovable. The cadet simply never showed emotion, leaving Nic still somewhat distrustful.

"Get up, now." Nic was brought into consciousness through a violent shaking of his bed. He looked up and saw Jones staring down at him. The clock showed three in the morning, a full hour before the usual time to wake up. *What does Jones want with me this time?*

"Outside," barked Jones.

The senior was waiting for him by the time he had dressed. Once out the door, he headed towards the team leader. "Time to show everything you have learned. The Lieutenant wants you to take the team out for a run this morning. Think you can handle it?"

"The Lieutenant?" Nic stammered.

"Yes, the man always at One's side. He feels you are ready to demonstrate leadership." His eyes narrowed. "Are you?"

"I can do it." Nic said with confidence.

"Good. Try not to embarrass me. I don't think you're ready, but it's not my call. Here, you'll need this." Jones pinned something on Nic's shirt. He looked down and saw the team leader's badge. "This will help them understand it's for real. Call them to formation this morning."

Nic had a full half an hour to consider what had just happened. The assignment of temporary team leader meant someone wanted to see all he had learned. His leadership skills would now be tested. Nic had seen several of the other teams recently, during the runs and workouts, with new leaders directing the others. He felt privileged to be chosen first from his group, but also wary.

Gathering the cadets for the morning workout proved to be more difficult than expected. Oni and Wang at first celebrated Jones' absence, guessing the senior must be occupied with a task. They looked forward to a substitute. In the past, other seniors were much easier on the group than Jones ever was. The silver pin caused Oni to pause, but only momentarily.

"Where did you steal that?" he asked sleepily.

"I didn't," Nic responded. "Jones gave it to me. Fall into line."

By the time Nic had roused everyone, it was already five minutes past the usual time to form up outside. Dodi had come to attention first, not questioning Nic's new authority. His eyes grew wide when he wakened and saw the silver leaf floating above him.

Standing in formation, several of the cadets smirked and even joked. Nic realized they were disrespecting him. The lack of an outside threat caused them to act in this manner. He realized order was necessary; otherwise the day would be a disaster. "Everyone, drop and give me thirty."

"What for?" Wang asked.

"I don't recall when we were out her last time so much talking," Nic replied. "Would you act this way if Jones were still here?"

"C'mon Nic, don't be so hard," Oni said.

Nic walked over to where Oni was standing and stood in front of him. "What if your life depended on staying quiet because the enemy was close by? Would you still be talking?" The crowd quieted. Oni grew thoughtful and looked straight ahead. *Good*, Nic thought. For the remainder of the day, there were no problems for the cadets standing at attention.

Nic Rocke   Marc Sherrod

Chapter Thirty-One

"I think I'm in love," Oni mentioned about a month after Nic had become leader.

"What?" Wang asked. He started to choke on his vegetables until Schneider slapped him hard on the back, sending a cucumber slice spinning across the floor. He continued to cough loudly and wipe tears away from his face until someone offered him a glass of water.

"Yeah, the new girl. The one that talks to you sometimes. She sure is cute. I wonder if we can ask someone out on a date here. Someone's got to know. Nic, you know everything here. How 'bout it? Think it's within the rules?"

A sting of jealousy burned within Nic at the thought of Oni's interest in Willow. He considered what he really wanted to tell Oni but thought better of it and attempted to act disinterested. He wondered if anyone could see through him. "No, it's not allowed."

"You sure? Oh, the rules suck anyway. I'm going for it. She's over there. The worst she can say is 'not interested.'" The boy batted his eyelashes and made a disapproving face, overplaying the part of a girl rejecting an advance.

As he stood, Nic grabbed his arm. "Sit down."

"Come on, it won't come to anything. Just having fun."

"Now." Oni looked at Wang, who shrugged, and indicated he better do as told.

"Dang Nic, you're made team leader and get all formal on us. I thought we were having a party here now. Guess not. Pretty crappy, right Wang?"

"Just take a seat," Wang responded, finishing his bowl.

"Great. Just great." Oni flopped down in his chair and folded his arms, irritated by the lack of support to approach Willow.

Several others from nearby tables heard the exchange and looked in their direction. As nothing more was said, they soon returned to their own conversations. Nic noticed Lauren was the last to avert her attention from the conversation. He locked eyes with hers, feeling her piercing, sharp stare. A condescending smile crossed her face. *She seems to be thinking we're all stupid.*

Nic hoped his teammates took the exchange as a new leader, eager to show his ability to recall policy and enforce it. As he looked around the table, the reactions of the team members seemed to suggest no one was harboring suspicions. Oni would be fine; sullen for now, but in half an hour he would be joking again, having forgotten the entire ordeal.

The Lieutenant stood in the background, a quizzical look on his face. He had observed the exchange and was staring at Nic. He said nothing to him as Nic passed by when the team rose and headed out for an afternoon workout.

Leading the group was becoming routine for Nic. Several days of running and workouts were replaced by small group puzzle-solving. He broke the group up into pairs to overcome various obstacles similar to the wooden bridge exercise where he had been injured.

As he approached a turn along their route, he noticed several canisters placed along the river bank. One was green, one blue, and the last yellow. The blue one was the largest and appeared to be the heaviest. Each had a small, flashing light on top. Curious, Nic called the group to a halt and approached them, cautiously. He asked Willow to join him.

"Can't be by accident," she mentioned. "I think the flashing is meant to catch your attention."

"Agreed," he responded. "But why?"

"I'll tell you." The voice from behind caused the two of them to wheel around. Jones stood on a small platform, towering above them, a defiant smile on his face. "In a few seconds the lights will begin to flash red. You will have ten minutes to transport all three canisters to the far side of the river. You will need to wade through it to get to the far side. Mind you, it's deep in several areas." There was more to the challenge than just this, Nic guessed. As if reading his thoughts, the senior continued. "You can only take two canisters over at a time. And," Jones smiled wickedly, "leaving the green and blue canisters together at any one time, or leaving the blue and yellow canisters together at any one time, will cause them to explode. In either case, you fail."

Nic was angry the senior would put his teammates in danger. "Is this something you came up with?" he asked. "I doubt One would think favorably of a *kay-det*, whatever his rank, putting others here at such risk."

Jones shot a look back at Nic, matching his angry stare. He climbed down the ladder from the platform and aggressively approached Nic. "Keep One out of this, Rocke. The canisters won't injure anyone if they explode. However, it is up to me to determine the penalty for failure. Several of your buddies over there could use a few days in quarantine."

"You wouldn't dare." challenged Nic.

"Why not? They've been getting overly confident these days. Some solitude will do them good."

"I'll tell the Lieutenant about this game you are playing."

"What, you think he'll believe you over me?" Jones gave a short laugh and became serious again. "Don't cross me on this. It's easy to make stuff up." The senior's voice grew quieter and his eyes narrowed. "I've been doing this for a long time and I've become quite good at it. Stop wasting my time. Get back to your group and figure this out." Jones shoved Nic backwards.

"What was that all about?" Willow asked.

"Come on. We have to get moving, fast." Nic's words seemed to trigger the canisters. An ominous, pulsing red flash replaced the benign, yellow light.

"Better hurry," Jones added, mockingly.

Nic formed his team around him. "Seems the easier part is determining who should carry what, and where," Nic observed. "Wang, you'll be assigned the blue one. It's heavy. I'll need two cadets each on those other canisters. You four," he pointed to several of the other team members, "we'll move the green and blue ones when the time comes."

"What about the river?" Willow asked.

"Right. Oni, scout ahead. Go check the river, you're quick. Come back and report the deep areas. We'll avoid those. Now the harder part," Nic sighed.

Figuring out the order in which to move things would be much easier on paper, he realized. Trying to visualize the solution in his mind was getting nowhere. After several seconds of inactivity, team members became anxious and began shouting solutions. It was impossible to concentrate. Only seven minutes were left.

Willow could see Nic's growing frustration. *If only they had a computer to run a simple solution,* she thought. Willow looked around her to see if the environment could offer any type of assistance. Her eyes stopped on Dodi, who was looking around absent-mindedly, completely unaware of their precarious situation. *Of course.* "Nic." She tapped his shoulder to gain his attention and pointed at the small cadet.

At first he didn't understand her intention. Then it dawned on him. *Maybe Dodi's brain circuitry is set up to handle logic puzzles as well as math.* He had to shout several times over the crowd to alert the boy. Dodi obeyed and waddled over to him. His large eyes looked upward, blinking once. Nic now had his full attention. Five minutes were left. "I need you to figure something out for me."

"Math?" Dodi asked, eagerness registering across his face.

"Not quite. I think you will like it, though." Nic looked back at the canisters and thought of the simplest way to explain the problem. "See the three canisters. Blue, green, yellow. We need to get them across the river, taking only one at a time. If we leave blue and green alone together, they explode. If we leave blue and yellow alone together, they explode. What do we do?"

He expected Dodi would need to take some time to process the information. The answer however came back instantaneously, as had the answers Dodi had given for the math problems when Nic first met him. "Take the blue one over first. Leave it. Then bring the green one over. Bring the blue one back. Take the yellow one over. Come back. Take the blue one over again. Done." With three minutes to go Dodi repeated his directions several times until Nic was convinced the plan would work.

"Wang, move, now. Take the blue one. Somebody, you there, help him. Oni, show him where to go." The large cadet moved over to the canister and hoisted it. A couple of the others managed to help him bring it to the water. Once Wang started across the river, Nic went through with Dodi each of the other steps one at a time. Time was running out, but the group was moving as fast as they could.

On the far side, Jones had a concerned look on his face. Estimating the time, Nic realized the team just might barely make it. He had to bark orders several times to the team, but they were following admirably. Only once did the group err by stepping into a deep area and lose the yellow canister momentarily.

With a minute to go, Wang lifted the blue canister one more time from the river bank and pushed it into the water. As he pushed from behind, several of the others pulled from the front.

Nic felt a swell of pride watching his team struggle as a unified group. Only a few months before, they were a collection of individuals who knew nothing about one another, let alone how to work together.

All the other cadets not directly involved in moving the canisters surrounded the small team and urged them forward. Nic waded into the river and joined the group. Wang grunted several times, giving the canister several violent pushes. As it rocked towards the beach, Jones walked towards the group. With a final heave, the group pushed the canister onto the shore, collapsing with it as it toppled onto its side. Jones screamed out that time expired. The cadets stood and celebrated, raising both arms and hugging each other.

"We did it!" Willow cried.

Oni had slumped to the ground in exhaustion. Wang raced over and with a celebratory shout threw him high in the air. Several others caught Oni. "Yeah, we made it," he replied weakly. A slight smile crossed his face.

"Yea! Yea! Yea!" Dodi swerved among the members of the group like a top out of control.

Nic surveyed the group. He had never been prouder of his team than at this moment.

When the noise died down, Jones addressed the group. "A valiant effort, truly. Only missed by two seconds." He looked at Nic with a smile of triumph. "As their leader, you need to decide who goes into quarantine. So, who will it be?"

Nic first thought the senior must be joking, having called time after the canister had reached the shore. Jones was unmoved, expecting an answer. "We made it. You called time after the canister was beached."

"No, I called time while it was still moving. It had not cleared the water line. Therefore, technically, you didn't complete the exercise successfully."

Several in the group screamed in protest, earning a deafening roar from Jones. In the silence, Nic felt his anger boil over. This was simply too much. As leader of his group, it was time to confront the senior. "You know we made it. Training hard, doing everything you asked. You pushed us, we responded. Look at us. I don't care what you say, in my mind, we won. Nothing you say can take that away. I'm proud of my team."

"What did you say?" The senior approached him, menacingly.

"You heard me. Don't act stupid. We know you see all, hear all. These games you play with us, putting us in impossible situations."

"I still need to know who you will choose for quarantine." demanded Jones.

"No, I won't do that. It's over. You want someone, fine. Take me. No one from my team is going to participate in this any longer. "We must have an audience with One," Nic demanded.

Jones studied him for a few seconds. The group watched the confrontation in silence. The senior's air of triumph and scorn disappeared. "I agree. Let's go see him now."

Chapter Thirty-Two

Nic and Willow looked at each other, surprise registering on both of their faces. They had expected complete rejection of the idea and dismissal. The walk to One's location gave Nic the time he needed to compose many questions. Willow seemed lost in her own thoughts, sometimes mouthing words in an unseen discussion. She was obviously as nervous as he was. The other cadets seemed anxious.

One emerged from the background of trees. His appearance was unchanged from the time Nic first met him.

"Sir, I can attest that my group has completed the initial phase," Jones began. "They have come together as a unit, demonstrating trust and mutual understanding. *Kay-det* Rocke has brought them together to perform as an efficient group. Just now, the last piece fell into place." Jones looked at Nic. His expression showed something not displayed before. Nic recognized it as a look of pride. "Self-sacrifice."

One nodded thoughtfully. "Mr. Jones, thank you for the assessment. I have monitored their progress and accept your observation."

Jones smiled to the group. "Good luck *kay-dets.*" Nic realized the senior had been playing a role the entire time. He wondered what Jones was really like.

"You have come with questions in need of answers. It is time to give them to you." said One. A nod of his head dismissed Jones. "Why am I here? What is this place? What happens after training? These are the questions circulating in your minds, are they not?" A patient, serene look crossed over One as he waited for them to compose their thoughts.

"Yes, those, and others." Nic responded. Willow's expression confirmed his answer.

"Fine. There is a lot of information to cover. I will be thorough." One looked up towards the sun and closed his eyes for a few minutes. He invited all of the cadets to sit down and continued. "You have stumbled upon the greatest secret kept from modern society. The world in which you have been living prior to your journey, and stay here, in essence, is a lie." Willow and Nic looked at each other. A growing fear was apparent in Willow's eyes. "Some of this you have already determined. Your first doubt came from the holo in the library. Oh, yes, I know about that," One smiled, "there is much we know about what has happened to you... out there. However," One continued, with a much more serious look as his eyes grew smaller, focusing on a point past the two of them; "much damage could have happened. We almost lost you to the Guardians on the platform. A lesser agent might not have had the sense of self-sacrifice that day."

Nic felt a pang of guilt run through him. The odd stranger who had given him the book must have known at some point the only way out for them was to divert the Guardians at the cost of his own life. Nic began to re-evaluate all he had come to think about the man.

"You have uncovered a secret put into place many years ago. Decades, in fact. It all starts with where your journey began. Dr. Stephen Butler. Many labeled his work inconclusive, even a failure. This could not be further from the truth. He was very successful."

"His work. Machines became smarter than us, didn't they?" The question from Willow cut to an area where Nic did not want to go. He realized however, that there was no going back now. The answer from One stabbed through the air.

"Yes. They also decided we were no longer capable of managing ourselves, so they took over. Everything."

"How could this have happened?" Nic asked.

One looked towards Nic, his eyes piercing through him. "How could it have not? This was not the first time we have allowed something else to make decisions for us. Man's creations are tools, nothing more. When we allow them to play a role greater than this, our ability to govern ourselves is compromised. It was only a matter of time, as we hadn't learned from earlier examples. We have now passed the point where not only our opportunity to determine our own lives has been affected, but the rights we have to make our own decisions simply have been taken away. Permanently."

Nic considered everything One said. Yet, there were still a few unanswered questions. "What happens in quarantine?"

The elder smiled at both of them. "We address people's problems."

"I don't understand," Oni said.

"Let me put it this way," One continued. "When you have had things in life that bothered you, who was there to listen?"

The question caught Nic off guard. "I've never thought of that before," he replied.

"Precisely. No one does. We live in an age where problems aren't addressed, but rather swept away, to be forgotten. Yet the problems just don't go away. Society's ways mask the issues, but they don't disappear. Medication hides the issues, making us feel better temporarily. Yet the issues lie there, latent, and show themselves in myriad of ways later in life."

"Why then, all the fear about quarantine?" Wang asked.

"It wasn't our original intention to make it this way," One replied, patiently. "Some mystique, however, has helped. After all, what would you have thought if you were sent to quarantine knowing that people were going to listen to you and help you sort out your issues? You might not take it seriously."

"*Kay-dets* who come back afterward do seem better, focused, more determined," Nic admitted.

"Because somebody is there to listen. For some of them, this is the first time in their lives someone else was there to believe in them." said One, with a nurturing tone to his voice.

"Why was Jones so tough on us? He isn't really that way, is he?" Nic asked.

"No, he isn't." One seemed to laugh, but Nic wasn't so sure. "But had he not been that way, you wouldn't have excelled to the level you did. You were forced to demonstrate your true potential under severe adversity. And you succeeded."

"So what do we do now?" Willow's voice sounded distant, almost inaudible.

"Yes, indeed. What do you do now?" One looked tired. Nic sensed a heavy burden was on the man.

"I, and a few others, most of whom have passed on already, created this base many years ago to try and do something about our unfortunate human condition. We have won a few battles, but the war is long. Out there, few have an understanding of what has happened. When it appears, as with all of you, someone comes to the realization of the true nature of events, we try to intervene. Unfortunately, we are often too late. We have our own methods of detection, but so does the enemy. Their resources are superior, their methods difficult to mitigate. Still, we have made some progress."

One managed a thin smile. His distant gaze focused again on both Nic and Willow. "This is where the two of you come into play. You will continue your training here until deemed prepared for return to society. You will join our organization's efforts to educate and to inform. The greatest strength a people can have is the gift of awareness. Without it, the people live as sheep, grazing unknowingly, unaware of the predators all around. Recognition of things as they really are is critical for our fellow citizens to awake from a drugged slumber and begin to make decisions for themselves again."

One stood. As the cadets turned to depart, he left them with a final comment. "This training, and the work yet to be done, is difficult. Anything of value in life usually is. As with my former colleagues, my time too will pass at some point, leaving the responsibility to you and your generation to continue the effort. I want to thank all of you for being here."

Chapter Thirty-Three

Nic considered all One had said the previous day during his early morning workout at the gym. Everything had begun to make sense. Jones treated him differently now. Nic had discovered earlier than most the purpose of the base and had been rewarded with confirmation of the truth.

"Just don't tell anyone outside of your team what you now know," Jones ordered.

"Why?"

"They're not ready yet. In time, they'll know, too."

A silence descended over the gym as Lauren entered. She was dressed in a black leather outfit which hugged the contours of her body. Nic was surprised. *I have not seen her in that before. She must have brought that with her... wherever she's from.* Mounting the parallel bars, she began an impressive routine. Her slender form moved seamlessly from one part of her workout to the next. Flexed muscles delicately changed the shape of her outfit. Activity stopped in the gym. All eyes focused on her. Even Dodi stopped what he was doing and watched. She seemed to notice and smiled, enjoying bathing in the stares. The girl dismounted and stood for several seconds, unmoving. Her arms were stretched high, pointing upwards. Her chest rose slowly to inhale. It was clear she was in fantastic condition.

She walked over to where Nic stood and smiled. "Hi." Nic mumbled a greeting in response. "Where's your girlfriend?"

"Oh, uh, she's not really my girlfriend. Really, well, more like a close friend."

"You don't sound so sure. Maybe you need to think about it." The girl's eyes bore through Nic. Her gaze held him. He wasn't sure how to answer.

"Yeah, I have." said Nic, weakly.

"Good. I'll be interested to know your answer when you figure it out." Lauren took a step closer, still holding him with her eyes. Nic found he couldn't break free. He felt both excited and captured at the same time; enjoying the attention, but also uncomfortable at the strength coming from Lauren. "You watch me a lot. I wonder why."

"Oh, sorry, didn't mean to. I won't do that anymore."

"Apologizing? That's interesting. Well, don't let me stop you. Do what you want, it's a free country. At least it used to be." Nic became increasingly uncomfortable. He knew that she could feel his growing uneasiness. She seemed to enjoy watching him squirm.

"I think you like what you see." she said with a sly grin.

He imagined he was caught in a giant, beautiful hand, the slender fingers wrapped around him, pressing inward. It alarmed him that he feared her, but more concerning to him was his attraction to her. Nic realized she was dangerous.

Her eyes softened and she stepped back. A slight smile crossed her face. *Victory.*

He felt she could read his thoughts, know his secrets, and even control him. He was helpless, facing such seductive power. "See you later… Nic." Lauren whirled and headed back to her routine, effortlessly. Nic felt exhausted.

Nic Rocke

Marc Sherrod

Chapter Thirty-Four

"Enough of this," Willow said. "You might have won over a couple on the team, but I see right through you."

"Really," Lauren responded, casually brushing back her hair with a dismissive tone. "So tell me, what is it that you see?"

"Trouble."

Lauren lifted her head and laughed. "That's it?"

"That's only the beginning. You have no interest in helping the team. All you care about is drawing attention to yourself. I don't know who let you in here, but it was a big mistake." Willow challenged.

Lauren's eyes flashed violently. Her smile was replaced by an ugly sneer. "I suppose you are here for nobler reasons. You think you're better than me?"

Willow's shoulders slumped. She became quiet but responded after a few seconds. "No, I don't. I'm still trying to figure all of this out. I don't feel I'm better than anyone."

"Good. For a minute there I thought you were getting ahead of yourself. In reality you are a sad, little girl, crying out for her lost parents."

Willow grew angry. She then realized the game. Her enemy was masterful at throwing someone off guard and belittling, then claiming victory. *This needs to stop. Now. I need to put my emotions on hold and deal with my anger later.* "You like to hurt people. Must make you feel superior. Tell me, when was the last time anyone showed a real interest in you? Beyond eyeing your body, I mean." Turning the tables on Lauren produced the intended result. Willow was not proud of what she said, but she needed to remove herself from Lauren's trap and take the offensive.

"How dare you." growled Lauren.

"You might think the boys on the team like you. I hear things, though. Remember reading about when people owned pets? Cats, birds, a lot of dogs. They had a term for the last one. 'Prized poodle.' A show dog. Prances around, getting all of the attention. Sound familiar?"

Lauren's eyes narrowed. Willow could feel the hate coming out of them. "Shut up."

Willow continued the attack. "What's wrong? Maybe I'm too close to the truth."

"You and I need to settle this." Lauren snarled.

There was danger in the direction this was heading. Combat with Lauren was unpredictable. Willow, however, didn't see an alternative. "Agreed. Tomorrow, then? The Kendo court. Before everyone gets up."

Nic Rocke Marc Sherrod

Chapter Thirty-Five

It was still dark when Willow woke up. She wasn't able to sleep well with the coming battle. Her sleep was disturbed with visions of the team members falling one at a time to Lauren's *shinai*. The last scene with Nic falling over jolted her to full wakefulness. Willow found herself panting hard. Sweat dripped from her forehead.

She rose and washed her face. Looking in the mirror, she resolved not to lose. If she did, Lauren would always be there to gloat, to remind her constantly, that she was superior. The other team members would never know of the battle. Lauren though, would never let her forget.

Beating her opponent would remove a threat to the team. She considered Lauren's presence distracting. Showing off by whirling her hair in the team's presence and moving her body in ways they had to notice forced their activities to come to a standstill. Putting Lauren in her place would stop this nonsense.

The team could then continue to progress, to come together as a unit.

Am I jealous of Lauren? In a general sense, no. If boys want to look at her, fine. In school, this happened often. There was always some girl or another around to attract the eyes of my friends. Willow looked at her image and realized she was kidding herself. She accepted Lauren's presence as a distraction, but she knew there was a deeper reason. *It's him. Who cares about the others? But I can't stand having Nic look at her that way.*

The truth had been there for a long time now. Training had taken her energy, and time. Just underneath the surface however, no matter what she was doing, her feelings lay patiently waiting for her to recognize them, and do something about them. Today was a good day to face her emotions.

She gathered her equipment and packed them into her bag. Looking at the *men,* she noticed the great number of scratches present. *Each one a memory,* she thought. On the left side was where Nic had struck her early in their training, his clumsy attack never quite hitting its target. A few painful bruises along the way had been testament to his inability to hit correctly. Recently though, he'd gotten much better.

As Willow was leaving, one of the girls turned over in her bed, forcing Willow to exit quietly, lest she wake the other girls and be caught. She realized the next time she would be back here would either be as victor, or vanquished. To Willow, losing was not an option.

When she arrived at the *dojo,* Lauren was already waiting. She appeared calm, unmoving. In *seiza* style, her legs were underneath her. As she approached the mat, Lauren stirred. The two faced each other. Willow bowed respectfully. Lauren barely dipped her head, a move many would regard as an intentional affront to an opponent. *Idiot,* Willow thought.

With *shinai* swords facing forward, the battle began.

Lauren was several inches taller, giving her a clear advantage for a *men* hit to the head. Willow would need to be prepared for this attack. It came, quickly. Willow was able to block it, but just barely. The sensor didn't register, meaning the hit was not clean. She tried to counter-attack to the wrist, but Lauren easily blocked the *kotei* attack. Willow realized Lauren had been watching her over the last few weeks and would be expecting these moves.

Willow moved to a *jo* stance by raising the *shinai* high over her head. This would allow her to attack to the top of the head more easily. Unfortunately, it also left her vulnerable. She was amazed at Lauren's ability to adapt. A side *do* swipe to her stomach forced Willow to peddle backward and bring her *shinai* down. Again, the sensor didn't register as the hit wasn't clean. Lauren grunted in frustration. Willow could see the anger pouring out of Lauren's eyes towards her. Lauren parried her *men* attack as easily as the earlier attack to the wrist. Willow realized something unorthodox was required.

Before Willow could next attack, Lauren shoved her hard, sending Willow crashing to the ground. "Sorry," she spat in mock apology.

Getting up slowly, Willow watched her opponent for a few seconds, looking for an opening. Lauren's *shinai* wavered slightly left and right, but not vertically. She would need to rely on an attack Lauren wouldn't have seen before. Timing her attack would be crucial. *Left, right, left right, left. Now.*

Willow started with a deliberate slow *kotei* strike which Lauren pushed to the side with little effort. As her *shinai* moved back left to resume its weaving pattern, Willow lunged forward with the rarely used *tsuki* attack to the throat. Lauren's eyes clearly showed surprise as the tip of the sword made contact, setting off the sensor. The block had come too late.

Lauren stood there motionless, still seething at the loss. Willow approached her, her voice barely above a whisper. "You and I have settled this. No more of your games. Leave them alone."

Chapter Thirty-Six

A great tearing sound could be heard coming from the far side of the camp. Nic looked in the direction of the noise and quickly shut his eyes as a flash of light pierced the night. Wasting no time, he called the group together and set off at a fast pace. As they drew closer to the source of the explosion, they could see several of the buildings now in a heap of rubble. A few cadets clawed their way out of the wrecked structures. Nic knew there must be several more inside.

"Oni, take three *kay-dets* and help that group over there. Looks like they need more strength to pull off the main door." With the remainder of his team, he continued forward.

It was clear the explosion occurred on the outskirts of the camp. *There's nothing out that way except for... One.* The area where the leader kept mainly to himself lay ahead.

"Double the pace!" Nic ordered.

"Where are we headed?" Wang asked, panting.

"See the smoke? Where else." The strong odor of burning wood filled the air. Nic expected to see the forest damaged, but the complete destruction of the location chilled him. Whatever had happened completely ruined this place.

Jones came up to the group. A severe gash cut across his face; blood was rushing from his head like a waterfall. The upper part of his shirt was already soaked. "We've got to get you help," Willow said.

"No time. I was in the building over there. What's left of it. Flying glass caught me." gasped Jones.

"What happened?" asked Nic.

"No idea." The senior winced several times. Clearly he was fighting a tremendous amount of pain. "Many *kay-dets* are still in those buildings."

"I know. I dispatched a few to start unearthing them." Nic responded.

"If the glass hit me from that direction, then –"

"The force would have come from over there," Nic cut Jones off. "My thoughts too. "One's location."

"Let's go. You, Willow and me. Three are enough to search. Besides, there are a lot of injured. Have the rest of your team help the wounded." Jones ordered.

"Right." Nic sent the others to search the remnants of the nearby structures.

It was difficult to find the glen where One made his appearances. The three had to backtrack several times before they were certain of its location. Shattered trees scattered the landscape. A strange quiet hung over the area disturbed only by the efforts of the others back at the base looking for survivors. "Who could have done this?" Jones asked.

"Isn't it obvious?" Nic replied. "Schneider. He volunteered earlier in the day to help One pack up the books." Willow nodded her head in agreement. It was clear Jones was wrestling with the idea. The senior cadet muttered something about Schneider.

"I never trusted that one, either," Jones concluded. "Never showed any emotion. Wouldn't be surprised if he wasn't human."

"Cyborg?" Nic asked.

"Maybe. It's getting harder to spot them now. Keep looking. There has got to be some evidence here somewhere. Schneider, or One, or… hey, where's Dodi?"

A panic overcame Nic. *Dodi. Was he also caught up in this?* The three headed in separate directions. Nic felt several times he had come across something useful only to find damaged trees and rocks. Several of the burning buildings were playing tricks on his eyes in the night.

Willow screamed. The sound was unmistakable to Nic. He rushed towards where he thought she must be. Jones found him halfway and the two ran together, vaulting over the broken terrain. They found her outside of a small hut, pointing inside.

"This is where he kept the books," Jones said. The two approached the entranceway cautiously.

"A body. In there, on the far side," Willow whispered.

As they entered the small structure, they could see a number of books strewn across the floor. The explosion had damaged the building but hadn't destroyed it. Brick and metal fell from the walls, making it difficult to progress further. With effort, the three helped one another traverse the destruction.

Someone was propped against the wall, unmoving. The force had knocked the person against the wall, leaving the limbs flopped in all directions, as if someone had discarded a doll. Nic and Jones looked at each other and proceeded. Taking a deep breath, Nic prepared himself to see the lifeless face of One, the man he had come to respect deeply during his time at the camp. As he turned the body over, shock gnawed through his body. Schneider's lifeless eyes gazed up at him. Clutched in his hand were Dodi's glasses. He took the glasses and examined them carefully. Stunned, he stepped back, bumping into Willow. "This can't be." gasped Nic.

"Nic, what is it?" Willow asked, alarmed. Nic looked again at the glasses and slumped to the ground.

Willow took the glasses and held them up, scrutinizing them. She turned them over several times. The lenses were made of a dense material and projected holographic images for the wearer. At the end of the frames on either side were small needles.

Jones joined her in examining them. "Oh, no."

"What is it? You two are really scaring me." stammered Willow.

"Those aren't glasses for humans. The display, the needles." whispered Nic.

"Then who would wear them?" asked Willow.

"A cyborg," Jones said, flatly.

****

Later that night Nic assembled his team. All members were crushed to find out the truth about Dodi. His masterful performance had fooled everyone. Oni openly wept at the news. Equally distressing to Nic were the assumptions he made about Schneider. Looking back, the cadet had never done anything wrong. He simply didn't show much emotion. Loyal to the end; he paid with his life to try and keep One safe.

"Where are they now?" Nic asked.

"Don't know. Dodi did a good job hiding his tracks." Jones looked away, seeming deflated. "At least I'm not sure. Someone might know but they aren't telling me anything."

Nic had never seen Jones so uncertain. The lack of any knowledge must be torture to the senior cadet. Worse would be if Jones understood someone knew the whereabouts of One and Dodi but purposefully withheld the information from him. "Look," Nic began, awkwardly. "You and I don't really see eye to eye on a lot of things. But we are in this thing together now. Hey, if I knew, I would tell you everything."

The change in Jones was immediate. His confidence recovered and he stood tall again. Nic was relieved to see Jones back to his normal self. "I believe you would, *Kay-det* Rocke."

Nic Rocke Marc Sherrod

Chapter Thirty-Seven

Everyone at the camp spent the next several weeks cleaning up. All told, over fifty cadets had died in the blast.

The daily routine of exercise and classes had been ruined. The Lieutenant took command of the base and had everyone openly discuss their concerns. It was amazing the progress they made on removing devastated buildings and salvaging those still useable. Keeping busy helped everyone's mood. Facing such adversity, the teams were resilient. In a short time, the camp was repaired, though the shattered woods were a physical and psychological scar; a daily reminder of the destruction. Nic believed the Lieutenant left the trees this way on purpose. The broken landscape daily recalled the guile of the unseen enemy, keeping the cadets on guard.

Nic had completed a morning workout when Wang rushed to meet him. Out of breath, he explained in gasps the Lieutenant wanted to see him. Clearly the news must be important. The man had never called for Nic before.

"Any idea why he wants to see me?" Nic asked.

"No clue. You know how he gets though when he wants you to have done something two hours ago? Yeah, that look. It's pretty serious, Nic."

Assembled where One's glen lay were all of the current team leaders. Nic recognized several of them through the morning exercises and several of the classes' team leaders only attended to learn directly from One. As he sat down, the Lieutenant began.

"The enemy is strong. We are bent, but not broken. You all are to be commended for your efforts. You have rebuilt the base and have kept your teams intact." All eyes remained fixed on the man. "I have some disturbing news I need to share with you. From these," he held Dodi's glasses high, "we have been able to determine the events of that night. We have deciphered several of the transmissions sent from these."

The Lieutenant looked deep into the eyes of each of the team leaders. Nic felt the man was talking exclusively to him.

"One has been stolen from us. He is alive, although at this point I can only guess what they are doing to him to reveal our operations. It's clear the danger is growing. We can't stay here any longer. I'm calling a general evacuation of the base. We will regroup on a future day and at a distant place. You will receive the details in a communique later. It's time now to talk with each of you about your specific next steps."

Nic waited in line as several of the more senior members talked with the Lieutenant first. Jones was grim-faced during his entire conversation, revealing nothing. Only once did a member look crestfallen, but quickly recovered from a hand on the shoulder and an assurance from the Lieutenant.

As the line whittled, Nic grew more anxious. Finally, it was his turn. "What's next?"

"I ask myself that every day," the Lieutenant responded. "There is so much to do." A tired look passed over the Lieutenant which he quickly dismissed. "You are to be commended, Nic. Good job in getting the cadets into teams yesterday and tearing down the barracks. We need leadership right now and you stepped up to the plate."

Nic smiled inwardly at the basebasket reference, finding irony in the reference to that which brought him to the "college" in the first place.

"What we do from here is disappear, for a while," the Lieutenant continued. "Besides, it's good for people to reconnect; see family, friends, even if it's just occasionally. Go back, see them. We will talk again in a few months."

Nic couldn't accept this decision. He had been through too much; put in everything he could here. There was no home "back there" anymore. His life was with the cadets now. "Why can't I be part of the transition?"

The Lieutenant hesitated, and then looked at Nic. A stark expression came over his face. "I... can't go into that right now Nic. I can only say it's best for you. In time you will know."

****

The dismantling of the camp began immediately. One's books were collected and packed into boxes. All evidence of the base had to be removed. All cadets were ordered to begin destroying the buildings. This bothered Nic greatly, but he knew there was nothing he could do to stop it. He approached the Lieutenant with apprehension and decided to speak first. "We have to find them. Both One and Dodi."

"Yes, we will Nic, but for now, your time here is done." said the Lieutenant, flatly.

"What do we do now?" asked Nic.

"You and Willow head back home."

"That's it? I don't want to go." Nic protested. "You must have some of the other team leaders doing other things. Let me join them."

"No, it's settled. You leave tomorrow. I will be contacting you in a few weeks. We will create a new camp and continue the fight. Sorry Nic, I have nothing more than that right now."

Chapter Thirty-Eight

Michael's family had been gracious in allowing Nic to stay with them when he returned. They were there to greet him as he departed the mag-lev platform. Nic had to create an entire fabrication of his experience, but only Michael continued to ask questions.

"Your team doesn't even have the new basebasket feedback screens?" he asked incredulously. "Everyone has them. Heard from some of the seniors, even Coach at our high school gave in and finally ordered them."

"Yeah, well, we don't have a lot of money, okay?" Nic shot back. The questions were becoming annoying.

It was clear that Michael was not buying the entire story, but he said nothing. Michael's parents were amazed at Nic's appearance. Nic mentioned the basebasket training had been

---

intense, though in telling the false story, his friend had a doubtful look on his face.

Everything seemed much smaller now to Nic. Recalling his experiences, he felt as if he were watching another person's history retold from a distant perspective. His return had coincided with the winter break, therefore a number of people were away on vacation. Bobby was somewhere back east. Connor as well, would be leaving soon for his family trip. When Connor mentioned a rural part of Texas, Nic clammed up. If he revealed too much familiarity with the region, it might cause suspicions to arise. He tried to talk with Connor, but they had so little in common now. Connor tried to show interest in his stories about "college," but it didn't last for long. Nic recalled last year when he went through the same experience with Tommy. He concluded that change caused people to move apart. While he wasn't angry, it did sadden him.

Willow took a different train back as part of an attempt by the Lieutenant to keep the cadets separate and avoid drawing attention to potential spies searching for them. Nic knew she was somewhere in the city, but her apartment had been rented to someone else. It was strange to see a married couple enjoying an outdoor barbecue from the veranda of her former home. Nic regretted walking by, but something had drawn him to see it for himself.

Everything has changed. At first I thought it was the world that had moved past me. The people, places. But really it's me who has changed. I know more now about what goes on… out there.

Before leaving the camp, Nic had been instructed by a senior cadet to refrain from logging onto the Screen or otherwise leaving a trail which would make it easy for the enemy to locate and track him. This forced him to take walks his first few days, but little more. He realized, at this pace he would soon grow soft, his body no longer having to endure the physical training regimen imposed for so long. He tried to keep in shape with occasional workouts, but it was not the same as being part of a team constantly training. Without much to do, he soon grew bored. *When is the Lieutenant going to contact me?*

"Nic." The voice called out to him, barely above a whisper. He had been on one of his walks to stave off boredom, but was having little success.

Nic approached the bushes. As he brushed back a few of the branches, Willow emerged. "I know we aren't supposed to meet, but I had to see you," she began. "So much has happened. I'm not sure how to feel anymore." Nic nodded in agreement. "What do you think will happen now?" she asked.

He looked around them at sights once familiar, now foreign to them. He thought of the start of the school year, and the increasingly strange adventures leading in many directions; returning them to of all places, back to where they had started. Yet it wasn't the same. It would never be the same again. They had seen too much, they had learned too much of what really was happening in the world. "I don't know what's next."

He expected to see her well up with tears, but none came forth. She had changed as much as he had. Perhaps in some ways, even more. The girl he once knew was now a young woman, confused but confident, scared but determined. He saw in her eyes what he felt inside himself.

She started to say something but he didn't hear. He touched her lips delicately with his finger as she had once done to him, stopping her in mid-sentence. He leaned forward, pressing his lips lightly against her mouth. At first she jerked in surprise, but soon relaxed. "I've been waiting all year for that."

"Yeah, me too," he responded.

Nic Rocke   Marc Sherrod

Marc Sherrod

Marc Sherrod started his career making video games. He has had the opportunity to work on a number of titles for several different companies, including both Sega and Sony.

More recently, he has had the opportunity to work in education. He served as a dean for an arts college and is currently a director for Media Arts programs at the college level.

Marc holds a Master of Arts in International Relations from Lancaster University (U.K.) and a Bachelor of Arts in History, with an East Asian emphasis, from Michigan State University. He is currently working on an M.B.A.

He has had the opportunity to live and work in Japan, study in England, and travel in both China and Taiwan.

36768431R00136

Made in the USA
Charleston, SC
18 December 2014